YESTERDAY'S
LIES

Cover Design and Layout: We Read Literary Services
Published by: TDUB Publishing
ISBN: 978-0-9831887-0-4
LCCN: 2010942107

Printed in USA

DEDICATION

To my grandmother (Nana) Marjorie Reid you were right. I do miss you more than words can express but your style, grace, and class live on within me each and everyday.

What lies behind us and what lies before us are tiny matters compared to what lies within us.

ACKNOWLEDGMENTS

I would like to thank God for all of the blessings he has given me. It's because of him that I'm able to make it through all the trials and tribulations of life. A special thanks to my mother Patricia Gadsden, my number one fan, and my role model. Mom you have ALWAYS believed in me and encouraged me to follow my dreams. When I grow up, I want to be just like you☺. To my children, Steven Antonio White, Jasmine Marjorie-Lynn Washington, and Jennifer Marie Washington thanks for all of your love and support. I also want to thank you for giving me a reason to push myself to make it to the next level everyday. My cousin Tonya Mason and my Aunt Donna Washington, you two were my first critics and it was your encouragement that pushed me forward on this journey. To my sisters Tanya and Michelle, thanks for teaching me how to share something very precious to me, my mom. My BFF, Maria, you know me better than I know myself sometimes. Thanks for all of your support and encouragement everyday for the past twenty-one years. To C Floyd, you and I will always have a special bond. No matter how much time has passed since we last spoke we can always pick up where we left off. Thanks to my good friend J Spriggs for believing in me and giving me my nickname, Tdub. R Wright thanks for bringing me back from a place I didn't belong, teaching me how to breathe again and giving me some great material for this book and others to come.☺ Thanks to R Singleton for surrounding me with your creative energy when I needed it the most. To everyone else whose path has crossed mine at some point in my life, thank you; everyone we meet touches our soul in a special way. I'm sure the time spent with you added something special to my life and I hope you felt the same about the time you spent with me.

Dear Journal,

Today I found out that Raymond the man I have been writing about for the past few months was a fraud. In fact, he is married to a woman whose self-esteem is so low she accepts the fact that he routinely cheats on her with other woman. She accepts this and has the nerve to feel sorry for us, the other women. I am in a deep dark place right now because I am hurting but I pray to God that I never become her. I want a man but I want a man of my own.

A love of my Own
One to call my own
Instead of always being alone
From time to time, I can borrow time
With one whose not mine or
One who only cares for their self
I am just another notch in their belt
What I thought I felt was just a momentary pleasure
The best I can do is sit alone
And see the blue all around me
Why is it blue, so blue in my world?
Cause no one not a one has ever
Been true to their word
Their actions and reactions proved
to be the exact opposite of what attracted me
A love of my own
Just one to call my own
And turn this lonely house into a home
So sad but true I'm so used to being without you
A love of my own
I don't think I could ever share
Myself, my space, my place with another
The fear of the pain is so clear
Too vivid the images of my own tears
Streaming down into the depths of my troubled, lonely soul
Too fresh are the wounds on my heart to even think that

I could part with my loneliness
Open up my heart put down my guard
Why is this so damned hard?
I just want to find a love of my own
One to call my own

6 MONTHS LATER

Chapter 1
Wednesday

The Girls

"So," I asked as soon as Toni made her way into the booth. Her butt had barely touched the seat before I started firing questions at her about her "lunch lunch" date earlier that day. Toni and I go way back to junior high school. We clicked right away on the first day of orientation and have been best friends ever since. This was our monthly girls' night out gathering at one of our favorite places, the Outback. We get together to talk girl stuff and catch up on each other's lives. Even though we both worked for the same company, in the same department, we rarely get time at work to talk like this. Each month we picked a different place, and we took turns choosing. This month was Toni's choice, and I was looking forward to next month already, because I knew exactly where I wanted to go. I want to check out this new place downtown, called Spice.

My girl Toni had a "lunch lunch" date today with the fine brother from accounting, Darien. This was not the first time they had hooked up but I was living vicariously through her. She was the single one. I, on the other hand,

1

was happily married with two children. A girl, Jayden and a boy, David, III (Tre), the best of both worlds, most people would say. My husband, David is the love of my life. We met during our first year in high school and have been together ever since. I cannot even imagine my life without him. He was my first and my only. I love to listen to Toni's stories about all the men she dates, only because it's so different from my life, not because I'm longing for something similar. This thing between her and Darien was becoming a regular thing, and I could not wait for the latest update.

"Girl," Toni started "it was off da hook. Not just the sex, I mean there was a connection."

"Toni," I said, trying to sound exasperated, and truly, I was. Every man she met was the one for the first week or so. "How much of a damned connection could there have been when ya'll only had an hour for lunch?"

"Jada," she continued, "I'm telling you there was a connection. The way he held me and looked into my eyes, it was like I was the only woman in the world."

"Toni," I said, chuckling while I picked at the food on my plate. "Let me ask you a question. You *were* the only woman in the room, right?"

"Of course I was!" Toni yelled.

"Ok, well, I was just checking, because you do some freaky stuff sometimes."

Toni reached across the table and swatted at me, but I dodged the blow and just smiled at her. "See, that's why I shouldn't tell you anything, because you never let me live it down. Seriously, though I know I've done some things in the past that I'm not proud of, and *yes,* some of them can be classified as freaky. I'm telling you not this time not with

2

him. We are taking things to the next level. We are going on a real date this weekend. He asked me out to dinner."

I rolled my eyes and said, "Well it's about damned time he spent some money on your ass. I mean, you've been giving him the booty, free of charge, for 4 – 6 weeks now."

Toni's faced changed, and I could tell my last comment hurt her and she said, "You sure know how to ruin a good time."

"I'm sorry, T, it's just that you're my girl and I love you, and I want you to find a man who treats you like you deserve to be treated. That's all."

She sipped her drink slowly and thoughtfully said, "I'm telling you Jada, Darien is the one."

The Guys

"Man, that girl is a real freak. She is down for whatever, whenever. I used to work through my lunch hour to make the day go faster so I could go to happy hour to try to pick up some women, but now I'm working it out with Toni during my lunch break, on a regular basis. I don't have time for any other women right now," Darien said, as I half-listened. We had been friends since elementary school. We became friends in kindergarten and played pee wee and midget football together. We started to go our separate ways in high school but always kept in touch and remained close friends. Shortly after we both graduated from college, we ended up back in the same boring hometown, Harrisburg, PA. There was no NFL contract for him, and I was still trying to break into the music business. When we met, we had sports in common, but over time it seemed like we really didn't have a lot in common at all, yet we kept in touch.

Darien was always bragging about his escapades with the ladies. He was supposedly a confirmed, until the day he would die bachelor; and I was in a long–term, committed, not quite ready for marriage, relationship. He teased me constantly about me being "sprung," or, as he liked to say, in jail with a life sentence. Therefore, I took this opportunity to tease him a little.

"So, Darien," I said, "you've been hitting that on a regular basis for awhile, now are you getting caught up or something?"

"Naw man, it's just a physical thing. I mean, the girl's body is on point, and I told you she is a freak. She has been down with the lunch thing for a while now, so she knows the deal. We did make plans to have dinner this weekend, though. I want to try some real freaky stuff, and need more than an hour to do what I wanna do."

I sighed heavily into the phone. "Darien, You're headed for another one of your heartbreak specials."

"Vince, what are you talking about, man?" Darien asked, sounding completely innocent.

"Don't act like you haven't seen the pattern, Darien. You meet them, sex them up, take them out, and then drop them like a hot potato. They end up heartbroken, and some have turned into that psycho-stalker chick, that all men hate. The constant phone calls, emails, text messages, why do you continue to put yourself in these situations, man?"

"Vince, I'm telling you, this one is different. She knows what it is."

4

"Ok then, so I will submit my nomination for you to be the player of the year then because I do not understand how you do what you do?"

"Vince, it's very simple you just have to be honest with them from the door. I told Toni on day one, when we first hooked up, that I didn't want a serious relationship. She said she understood and she wasn't looking for anything serious either."

"Well man, seems like you have it all under control, so I'm not going to say another word about it. I got to go man. I'm meeting my girl, Gina, for dinner tonight."

"Alright man, tell that fine-ass girl of yours, I said hello."

"Man you better cut that out; don't even be looking at my girl like that."

Darien laughed and said, "You know I'm just teasing you man. I'll holla at you later."

Chapter 2

Saturday

The Guys

"Darien," I asked, "did you decide where you were taking Toni for dinner tonight yet?"

"Yes, I decided to take her to the Hibachi steak house. I was thinking about what you said. I want it to be a nice restaurant because I do not want her to think I'm cheap. I also do not want it to be too intimate so she thinks it's a romantic date or anything. You know at those places you usually sit with six or eight other people at the table. It's kinda hard to get into a real deep conversation with all those other people around".

"Man, you have it all figured out don't you?"

"Yes, I do," he answered confidently.

I continued to probe. "So did you figure out how you're going to transition from dinner to all that freaky stuff you've got in your head? Did you decide your place or hers yet?"

"I'm not sure man. I mean I cannot decide if I want to go to her place so that way I can leave whenever I want. Or my place so it's on my turf, if you know what I mean."

7

I shook my head and said "Man why are you making this like a game or something? You said you just want to spend some more time with her, getting freaky, right?"

"Yes"

"Ok, so if you have been up front with her about your intentions, then it should be simple. You go out to eat and then you simply look her in the eye and say, your place or mine? What is so difficult about that if you're being honest and you both know the deal?"

He thought for a minute and then answered, "Yeah, I guess you're right. It's simple. We are going to go to her place so I can get *outta* there as soon as I'm finished doing what I do." he said, in a matter of fact tone then continued. "That just means I'm going to have to pack my supplies and put them in my trunk."

Although he could not see me, I was shaking my head. "You're too much man. You know one day a woman is going to flip the script on you, get you caught up, and then drop *you* like you have been doing to *them* for years. Turnabout is fair play".

I imagined he was shaking his head now. "That's NEVER gonna happen man. I'm not going to get caught by any woman. Toni is a nice girl with a hot body but that's it. There is no love connection going on."

The Girls
Jada

"Jada," Toni screamed into the phone "What should I wear?"

I let out a heavy sigh and said, "Toni, why are you so worried about your clothes?   Darien has already seen all there is to see on you right? I mean ya'll been hooking up for over a month now."

Now it was her turn to respond with a heavy sigh. "I know J, but this is our first real date and I want it to be special. I want him to only notice me in the room."

"Ok girl" I continued. "So where are you guys going anyway?

"We are going to the Hibachi Steak House."

"Wow, that's a nice place for a first date. Not cheap at all."

"I know, I told you we were taking things to the next level. He is not cheap and he knows how to treat a woman. The only thing I do not like is the atmosphere. It's not very private. You know how you sit at those big tables with six or eight other people. I was looking forward to some alone time to talk to him about us."

I thought about the last time I had been there and tried to remember the layout of the restaurant. I knew she was right about the big tables around the hibachi grill, but I was trying to recall if there were any private more intimate tables also. "Toni, I think you might be able to request a private table away from the grill."

"Really?"

"Yes I think so. So what is the plan? Are you meeting there or is he picking you up?" Sounding preoccupied, Toni said, "Huh? I mean, umm, he's picking me up."

"Girl what are you doing?"

"Oh I'm still trying to figure out what to wear."Listen, Toni, we can only solve one problem at a time. Stay focused ok?"

"Ok"

"So he's picking you up and you're going to the restaurant together so you have some time in the car to talk right?"

"Yes that's true,"

"You have two options. You can call the restaurant to request a private table now, or you can discuss it with him on the way there and see what kind of vibe you get from him."

"Yes, you're right. I think I will go with the second option. He made the arrangements, so I don't want to mess up his plans by calling the restaurant and changing anything."

"Yeah, you're right that wouldn't be good. Ok so now onto our next problem, what to wear? Why don't you wear that cute little black sundress you bought the other week?"

"I always wear black, Jada. I wanted something with a little more color."

I racked my brain trying to remember Toni's wardrobe and what colors look good against her caramel complexion. "I got it, wear that red scoop neck sleeveless blouse and your black capris. You know red is your color."

"Yes" she enthusiastically agreed. "That's perfect girl. That's why you're my *bestest* friend in the whole wide world and you're going to sing at my wedding."

I could feel her wide smile through the phone. Then a shiver ran down my spine. Toni was really feeling this guy and I was afraid it was going to be another heartbreak for her. She has not been lucky in love. Partly because she always gives too much of herself too soon and people take advantage of her. Me on the other hand, everyone I meet starts at zero and has to earn my trust. I only saw Darien in passing at work. I didn't really know him but if this thing between him and my girl continued, we were going to have to talk. I only needed five minutes with him to determine if I thought he was worthy of Toni or not. Time would tell, but for tonight, she was happy and so was I. "Ok Toni well go ahead and finish getting ready. I will see you tomorrow at the Hilton for brunch. You can tell me all about your wonderful date then."

"Yep girl I will be there at eleven sharp. See you tomorrow. Bye".

Toni

My doorbell rang right on time, and as usual, I was running late. I still needed to put the final touches on my hair and makeup. I peeked out of the window and saw Darien standing there all 6' foot 4' of him, looking fine as hell. My heart skipped a beat when I thought about our lunch date the other day.

"Focus Toni." I said aloud to myself. Tonight is about getting to know Darien and building a relationship, not sex. You have already taken care of that part. I have to stop building my relationships backwards. I always get to the sex part first and that's a problem. The doorbell rang again. I rushed down the stairs and opened the door.

"Come on in Darien, I have a few more things to attend to and then I will be ready. Make yourself comfortable in the living room and I will be right back."

"Ok," Darien said and headed towards the living room.

Darien

I knew exactly how to get to Toni's house since it had been the scene of the lunch dates over the past month or so. As I parked and approached her door, a strange feeling came over me. I do not know why but Vince's words about this being another heartbreak were in my head. I could not understand why, but some of the things he said to me bothered me. I had been honest with Toni up front about what this was, and what it was not. I know she heard me. She is a smart woman. I shook my head to get these thoughts out of my mind. I rang the bell and waited patiently for her to open the door. When she did, she blurted out something about not being quite ready yet, and directed me to the living room. I did get a quick glance at her before she disappeared and she looked great. I mean, I've seen her before, but tonight she looked a little different. I guess I was used to seeing her dressed in business suits at the office.

Toni

The drive to the restaurant started quiet. I had so much I wanted to say but I was trying to be polite. Darien seemed a little bit more uptight than usual. We actually had never been alone together like this. We usually drove separate cars for our lunch dates. He was playing Kenny Lattimore, one of my personal favorites. Initially we chit - chatted about some of the office gossip. Then when there was a brief silence, I asked, "Darien have you been to the Hibachi Steak house before?"

"Only once or twice, why do you ask? Would you like to go somewhere else?"

"No," I replied, "It's a very nice place but I'm not sure I like the fact that we will be sitting with so many other people at the same table."

Darien

Oh my goodness. Here we go. She wants to be alone so we can talk. Damn it! This is not going according to my plan at all.

"I'm pretty sure we could request a private table if you would prefer."

Please let her say that's okay, I'm not in the mood for this intimate "get to know you" crap tonight. I already know how I want this to go down and this is appearing to be headed in the wrong direction. Why do women do this? She told me directly she was not looking for a relationship when we hooked up. So how in the world did I get here, on my way to a dinner date? This is not what I signed up for at all.

Toni

Yes, I would rather be alone with you Darien, I thought to myself, but instead I said, "No you don't have to go out of your way to make any special arrangements. It's a Saturday night and they're probably busy anyway. Let's just stick to the plans you made and we can be alone later, after dinner."

Darien

Yes, that's what I'm talking about, alone after dinner. That's what I'm looking forward to as well, I thought to myself, as well pulled into the parking lot of the restaurant.

"The parking lot looks pretty full, let me drop you off at the door and then I will park and meet you inside."

"Ok," Toni said and she gracefully slid out of my black Nissan Altima.

I stole a glance at her plump backside and smiled to myself as I thought about my after dinner plan. Then I said aloud, "yep tonight is going to be one hell of a night Ms. Toni."

Chapter 3

Toni

"Dinner was great Darien. I'm always impressed with the chef and all the tricks they do while they prepare the food."

"Thanks Toni I'm glad you enjoyed it."

"So the night is still young do you want to go back to your place or would you like to go somewhere else?" Darien asked.

I nibbled on my bottom lip a minute, thinking before I responded. I wanted to be alone with him so we could talk. I knew if we went straight, back to my place we would end up in the bed. I was ok with us ending up there eventually but it was only 9 pm so we had some time.

"Let's take a ride down by the riverfront."

"Ok that sounds good. We can take a walk, to walk off some of that dinner we just ate."

"Perfect"

We rode in silence listening to music both lost in our own thoughts for the rest of the ride to the riverfront. I was thinking about all the things I wanted to ask him, but I didn't want it to sound like I was taking an application or anything. I mean up until tonight all of our time together was spent in the bed with very little talking. I really didn't know much about him and I wanted to.

Darien

I was kinda' glad Toni suggested we go somewhere else before heading back to her place; although my plan was, to wine and dine her then get straight to the point, which was desert and she was on the menu. I was getting a different vibe from her than before. Dinner was nice. We made light conversation with each other and the others at our table. The way she ate and carried herself intrigued me. I found myself wanting to talk to her more right now. When we arrived at the river, I found us a nice parking spot, and we got out to start our walk. At first, we walked along in silence just listening to the water and enjoying the gentle breeze blowing around us. I decided to start the conversation, since it seemed she was going to allow me to take the lead, and this was something I liked. Too many women try to lead a brother around most of the time by the nose, and I definitely was not feeling that.

"So Toni," I started, "How long have you been in sales?"

"I started right out of college. I got a job working for American Health Products as an intern right out of college. So how about you, what brought you to this wonderful little city of ours?"

"I was born and raised here and came back home after college."

Toni

Damn. I just insulted him and didn't mean too. I didn't know he was from here. I just assumed some unfortunate twist of fate landed him here as it did for me. I tried to think fast so I could recover. "Wow, I didn't know this was your hometown. So, where did you go to college and why did you come back here?"

Darien laughed and then said, "Well I went to University of Pittsburgh and I came back because this is where my family is. Honestly, I never thought I would end up back here. When I left for college, I was optimistic of getting an NFL contract or something like that. However, God had other plans for me. I wanted to be close to my mom and my younger sister, so I came back shortly after college. You sound like you really don't like it here."

Damn, I was caught, I thought to myself. "Well Darien, it's just that I'm from DC, so after being raised there this seems so *small town* to me."

"Yes, it is, but my mother always said it's a great place to raise children."

Oh great, I thought, *he wants to have children someday. That's a plus.*

He continued "I'm not planning on having any kids, anytime soon, if ever. I'm just saying what my mother always said."

Wow, I thought, *cancel that plus on the kid thing*.

17

Darien

Why in the hell did I just say something about raising children? What is wrong with me? I must be losing my mind. I'm not thinking about having children anytime soon. After this exchange we walked along in silence for a while longer until she said, "Darien so what are we doing here?"

Oh. My, I thought, here we go. Everything was going along just fine, and I really wanted to avoid this conversation. "Toni," I started and stopped walking I turned to face her. "I thought you understood what was going on here? We are two adults who enjoy each other's company. We've spent some time together over the past few weeks..."

"No Darien," she interrupted. "We've had sex together that's it. We have not spent time together."

"Well Toni, isn't that spending time together, too?"

"I guess technically it's, but not really," she said, then continued, "spending time together is like this, having dinner, talking etc."

"Ok," I said. "I agree this is more like spending time together, so maybe that was a bad choice of words. I thought we both were attracted to each other and decided to act on that attraction. Is that a better description?" I asked.

"Yes I think that's more like it."

Toni

I'm getting that feeling again, like I've made the same mistake again. Getting physical too soon and ruining the potential for a meaningful relationship. Tonight has been nice and I do not want it to end on a sour note, so I need to pull this conversation back a bit.

"Darien tonight has been wonderful so far. I enjoyed dinner and we did get to spend some time talking and getting to know each other. Let us leave it at that for now. Ok?"

He looked relieved and said, "Yes Toni I would like that. So are you ready to head back to your place?"

"Yes," I said and we turned and headed back towards his car. The ride back to my place was very quiet. I was certain I had ruined the entire evening with my big mouth. We pulled up to my place and he hesitated for just a minute after he parked.

Then he turned to me and said, "I understand if you want me to go home after our talk."

"No, its okay. You can come in for a little while if you want to."

"I actually packed a bag because I had planned on staying with you all night."

That was the music to my ears. I smiled and said, "Then let's stick to what you had planned." I leaned forward to plant a kiss on his lips. We kissed for a few minutes and then I turned and started to open my door.

"Please," he said. "Allow me to open the door for you. After all, you're a lady."

Yes, I am. I thought to myself and patiently waited for him to exit the car and come around to my side to let me out. So maybe I had not ruined the evening after all. Things seemed to be back on track.

We were barely inside my front door before he was all over me. Okay, wait, maybe I was all over him. Not sure but all I know is we were all over each other. This was very

19

similar to our lunch dates, but then all of a sudden he stopped and pulled himself away.

He said, "Let's go upstairs and get more comfortable."

"Okay." I was somewhat prepared for this. Before we left for dinner, I had taken the time to prepare my bedroom and bathroom just in case this is where we ended up. I had candles all around my room and my bathroom. When we entered my room, he excused himself to the bathroom. While he was in there I lit the candles in the bedroom. I also turned on my *iPod*, and again being prepared, I had created a new play list specifically for this occasion. Then it was my turn in the bathroom. I lit the candles around the tub and sink. Then I slipped into my red teddy and thong set, that I recently purchased for a special occasion like this.

Darien

While Toni was in the bathroom, I grabbed my bag and started to pull out some of my special treats I had packed. As I looked around the room at the candlelight and soft music, my sex toys seemed a little out of place. I decided to leave them in the bag. I pulled out my box of condoms and my flavored oil and put them beside the bed. I stripped down to my boxers and waited anxiously for Toni to return. I was feeling the whole candlelight and soft music vibe. This was very different from our lunchtime encounters. This was going to be a long night. Just then, the bathroom door opened and in the candlelight, I saw her silhouette, as she stood in the doorway looking at me. Her body was perfect, curves in all the right places, not too skinny and not too heavy. She was just right. She was wearing a very revealing red teddy. I sprang to attention immediately. It was weird. I had had sex with her many times, but right now at this very moment, I felt very nervous. I was not sure what my next move was going to be.

Toni

I opened the bathroom door and stood in the doorway looking at Darien lying across my bed wearing only his boxers. When he saw me, he sat up straight, and looked like his mouth was hanging open. I chuckled, as I thought to myself, why is he acting like this is the first time he has seen me almost naked? I wanted this night to be special, different from our lunch encounters, where we were always watching the clock. I wanted to take it slow and I wanted him to be in control. I know men like that. I slowly walked toward him and stood by the side of the bed next to him. He reached out and grabbed me to pull me closer to him, until his face was resting right in between my breast, which were partially exposed. He gently inhaled my scent, then turned his head, and gently kissed each of my breasts. Then he stood up, lifted me up, and gently placed me in the center of the bed. To my surprise, he climbed onto the bed and lay next to me facing me. At first, we were not touching and he just looked into my eyes. I was getting nervous. I felt like I could hear myself breathing. It sounded very loud. It seemed to go on forever so I said, "Darien is everything ok?"

"Yes Toni," he said. "Everything is fine. It's just that I want to take my time and really get to experience all of you." I felt myself blushing. He continued, "I know you have enjoyed our lunch time hook ups, but this is going to be different. A much better experience I promise you."

He leaned towards me and started to kiss me gently at first, and then with more passion and intensity. He slid his lips down to my neck.

Oh, my GOD. I thought, *That's my weak spot.*

"Hmm" I moaned.

He continued south to my breast, stopping to pay special attention to each one. In one smooth effortless motion, he lifted my teddy over my head. He continued planting soft sensual kisses down my stomach. When he got to my thong, he grabbed it with his teeth and I slowly raised my legs to allow him to remove it. I'm not sure when he took his boxers off but now we were completely naked, and he moved back up to plant sweet kisses on my lips. He lay on his back and pulled me over to rest my head on his chest. We lay there listening to Leona Lewis' rendition of *"The First Time ever I saw your face,"* a remake of the old Roberta Flack classic. After the song was over, I do not remember the next or any song after that. Darien began to do things to my body that I never imagined were possible.

Chapter 4

Darien

I woke up startled. I didn't recognize my surroundings right away, but then I heard Toni's voice. She was singing, and I remembered where I was. Her voice didn't sound half-bad, I thought to myself. I might have to mention that to Vince. He was always looking for good talent. He aspires to break into the music business. My boy had mad talent and he was determined to make it. I lay there for a minute trying to remember as much as I could about last night. The memories brought a smile to my face. Then horror set in. Oh my, it's the morning and I'm still here. I was supposed to be gone when she woke up. That was the plan. Sex her real good, and then leave before she woke up. Just as I was reviewing my foiled plan, Toni walked into the room carrying a tray.

"Good morning, sleepy head," she said. "I fixed us some breakfast. Wasn't real sure what you liked, so I made a little bit of everything."

The food smelled wonderful and I was hungry. I was stuck on the word "*us*" in her statement. Even though this was not a part of my plan, I decided I was already way past where I wanted to be with this, so I might as well play along. What was I going to tell my boy Vince? I cannot tell him that I stayed the entire night and got served breakfast in bed. I will never live this one down if he finds out. I'm going to have to play it cool with him, like the night ended up the way I told him it would.

"Thanks Toni," I said. "Everything smells wonderful."

Toni

I woke up early and Darien was still sleeping. I slid out of the bed trying not to wake him, so that I could go and make breakfast. Again a part of my plan, I had everything I needed to make a breakfast fit for a champion. Eggs, bacon, sausage, ham, pancakes, fruit, and I even squeezed some fresh oranges for juice. I really enjoyed myself last night and I wanted him to know how much I enjoyed his company. My mother always said that the way to a man's heart is through his stomach. I hope she was right because I really put some effort into this. I actually love to cook, but it's no fun cooking for one person. Darien really seemed to be enjoying the food. So much so, in fact, we were not talking at all. He focused on eating and I focused on watching him eat. This man was gorgeous. The way his muscles flexed when he moved his arm to pick of the food, I could see the strength in his arms. Those same arms that held me tight last night and put me into positions I had only heard about. He also had a killer smile, with the most, perfect straight, white teeth I think I've ever seen in my life. Yep, I thought to myself he is worth keeping.

Darien

The food was excellent. Toni can really cook, I thought to myself, as I finished the last of my pancake. Toni was doing the traditional picking at her food and eating like a bird thing that women do when they're getting to know a man. That made me smile.

"Aren't you hungry?" I asked.

"Not really, I usually don't eat this early."

"Oh," I said, "I thought you were doing that eating like a bird thing that women do when they first meet a man."

She laughed and said, "No, That's not my style. If I'm hungry, I'm going to eat no matter who is watching. Remember last night at the restaurant?"

"Yep, you're right," I said. "You did throw down last night. I forgot about that."

I laughed and she blushed and said, "Hey I'm not shy. Everyone has to eat, right?"

"Yes they do," I said.

After I finished eating Toni offered the use of her bathroom for me to take a shower and change, which I did. While I showered, I thought about the entire evening and how I really enjoyed myself, even though things didn't go totally according to my plan. I found myself wondering what was next. I knew our lunch date days were over. I had not thought about the impact having dinner and a sleepover would have on our afternoon sessions until now. Clearly, I had not thought this through before I made this move. I was thinking that maybe, I went a little overboard with all the holding and caressing. I mean I know women like that stuff, but that's not my style. I felt like I had done everything wrong, but I still felt good, which was very strange for me. I had to get out of here so I could go home and get my head straight.

Toni

While Darien was in the shower, I snuck downstairs to call my girl Jada. We had already planned to meet for brunch today, so I could fill her in on my date with Darien. Since it turned into a sleepover and breakfast, I had to push back our meeting until after noon. Jada was excited that it turned out so well, and glad that I had pushed our lunch date back. She had agreed to meet me at 11, but she really likes being able to attend church every Sunday with her husband and kids. Now that we were not meeting until one, she could do that.

Darien finished up in the bathroom and came out looking like he stepped off the cover of GQ magazine. He seemed a little different after his shower. Awkward, maybe, was the best way to describe it. He seemed unsure of how to say goodbye as we stood in my doorway. I had been letting him take the lead up until this point so I decided to help him out a bit.

"Darien, I had a really great time, and I'm looking forward to spending time with you again. You have my number, so just give me a call, okay?"

"Yeah, sure," He stammered. "I had a great time, too, and I will be in touch soon."

I started cleaning, first the kitchen and then I put my room back together. I showered and got dressed to meet

Jada. As I was getting ready, I was thinking about my night with Darien, and trying to put my thoughts together, so I could accurately express how I felt about everything to Jada. She loves how I express myself. She says I'm overly dramatic about everything but she loves it. It keeps her coming back for more.

I really admire Jada. She is a great friend and a wonderful mother. I often watch how she is with her kids, and I hope that one day when I'm a mother, that I have the same patient loving relationship that she has with hers. I was also a little jealous of her loving relationship with her husband David. They were meant to be together. They met in high school and have been together ever since. He was her first, and only, and their relationship seemed perfect to me, an outsider, looking in.

Just as I started to head out the door to meet Jada, my cell phone rang. I glanced at the caller ID and although the number seemed vaguely familiar, I didn't recognize the number. It was an out of state number too. Hmm, I wonder who this is, I said to myself, but quickly decided to let it go to voice mail. I was on a mission, to get to Jada to tell her all about my evening with Mr. Wonderful.

Darien

On the ride home, I continued to think about my evening and morning with Toni. I really had some explaining to do. Good thing I didn't have to worry about hearing from Vince until later today or even tomorrow. His girl, Gina, always had him tied up on Sundays. First in church and then at her families house for dinner. They were basically married, which is why I do not understand why they just do not go ahead and get married. He has been exclusive with her for almost three years now. They still have their own places, but they spend almost every night together alternating between their two houses. The accountant in me thought this was silly and a waste of money both of them paying mortgages and utilities, when they were always together anyway. However, as Vince would say, it's none of my business, so I stay out of it. When I really thought about it, I thought I was the last person in the world to be giving anyone relationship advice. My track record with relationships was not good. In fact, I do not think I ever had one last more than a few months. I would get bored, or they would start to want more commitment than I could offer so we would go our separate ways. Most of the women could not make it past my *thirty-day test*. That's where I try to have sex with them every day for thirty days straight. I was a highly sexual being, and my partner needed to be also. If she could not hang with me for a full month then she was not worth my time. I wonder how Toni would do with sex, every day, for thirty days. I was not sure if I was ready to try it on her. She was different, and I had to figure out what my next move was going to be.

The Girls
Toni

"Toni," Jada called, "over here." She said as she waved me over to the table she had reserved. I was glad we decided to meet at the Hilton downtown. They have a very good Sunday brunch. I laughed to myself as I thought about the breakfast I had made for Darien earlier, but had not eaten. When I reached the table, Jada was stuffing another piece of muffin into her mouth. For the life of me, I could not understand how she ate so much, but remained so thin. It drove me nuts. My body was in shape but I had to work out on a regular basis to keep it this way. I started to sit down but Jada stopped me and said, "Girl, go ahead and get you a plate now. I want to hear all about your evening and I do not want to have to wait for you to get food."

I threw my purse onto the chair and said, "Order me a glass of water with lemon and a small cranberry juice." as I hurried towards the buffet. Being conscious of my figure, I resisted the urge to go for the fattening foods and concentrated on the fruit, cottage cheese, and yogurt.

When I got back to the table Jada asked, "Toni, why do you eat like you're scared to gain a pound?"

I watched as she stuffed the rest of her muffin in her mouth.

"Well Jada," I stated in a matter of fact tone, "not everyone was blessed with your metabolism. Some of us actually do gain weight based on what we eat."

Jada responded with a chuckle, "Why, are you hating on me girl?" I just rolled my eyes and started on my fruit and cottage cheese meal.

"So where do you want me to start?"

Jada quickly said, "Start with the juicy stuff." I laughed and put another spoonful of food into my mouth. While I did this, Jada thought again and said, "No I want to know what was different about this than every other time you two have been together, except for the actual *date* part."She emphasized the word *DATE* on purpose.

"Well," I started, "for one we spent more time talking than ever before. We talked in the car on the way to dinner.

We also talked a little during dinner and the best part was the walk along the riverfront we took after dinner"

"Oh, that sounds good," Jada, responded in between bites. "What else?" I was hesitant to give her details, and I was not usually like this. "What's wrong Toni? Why are your holding back on me now?"

"I guess I feel a little funny talking about this with you right now. I mean it is Sunday morning and you just came from church."

Jada laughed and rolled her eyes then said, "Girl, you know half of the people I was in church with this morning were doing far worse things than you did last night. Hell, some of them came straight from the club or doing their dirt to the church. So, girl, please just spill the beans."

I was cracking up and then leaned in closer to Jada and said, "All I can tell you is if I'm going to hell because of what I did last night the trip there would be well worth it."

Now she was laughing so hard she couldn't breathe. Jade always says I'm so dramatic about everything so she knew this was going to be good.

I sat back in my chair and said, "Well our time in the bedroom was less rushed obviously. It felt more like two people who were attracted to each other and less like two wild animals who couldn't control themselves."

Jada laughed and almost spit her juice all over me. I just know she had a mental picture of the animal channel and two wild animals letting nature take its course. She said, "enough about wild animals, I want to know if you still think Darien is the one."

I didn't answer right away, which was odd for me. I took a minute and thoughtfully answered with a smile, "Yes I do Jada. There is something about how he makes me feel that's different than anything I've ever felt. I can't describe it."

The look on Toni's face told Jada that she was dead serious. Jada knew right then and there that she had to meet this guy and get her own read on him. Her girl, Toni, was in deep and she was not going to sit by and watch her get her heart broken again. Jada's heart could not take another Toni heartbreak. Jada's husband, David, could not survive another one either. They had both been through so many of these with Toni. Her husband was affected because Toni's heartbreaks always resulted in Jada being away from her husband for days on end, while she nursed a distraught Toni back to sanity. Jada loved Toni to death, but Toni was one dramatic person. Toni loved hard and deep.

"Jada, Jada," I called.

"Yes," Jada finally responded.

"Where did you go? You have been staring off into space for the past few minutes. What's wrong?" I asked.

"Oh nothing T, I was just thinking about what you said about Darien, about him being the one."

"Oh," I said and hung my head. "You're thinking I'm setting myself up again don't you?" I asked.

Jada was afraid that's what was happening, but she didn't want to hurt her feelings, so she said, "No actually I was thinking that I need to meet him soon before you start planning the wedding."

I laughed, and faked as if I was going to throw my napkin at her. Jada wanted to keep the mood light, but she knew what she had to do as soon as she got to the office tomorrow.

Toni was so dramatic and expressive, she always kept a journal, and she wrote in it almost everyday, religiously. Jada wondered if Toni had started a *Darien journal* yet.

"So, Toni have you been keeping up with your journaling?" She asked.

"No, Jada, I've not started a *Darien journal* yet," I answered.

"Oh, I was just wondering. Did you write anything about your date with him?"

I smiled at her and asked, "You know me well, don't you?"

"Yes, I do." she said with a wink and a smile.

"Yes, I gave him an honorable mention in my entry last night," I said, then continued, "I'm actually a little nervous about writing anything about him in my journal."

"Why is that?" She asked.

"Well, I guess it's because I usually write all this stuff about guys and then when I go back and look at what I wrote, I always feel so silly or ashamed. I really do feel something different about Darien and I don't want to jinx it."

"I guess I can understand that." Jada replied.

The girls continued their meal, started to talk about the kids and David, and then briefly caught each other up on the recent office gossip. Jada was wondering how Toni was able to keep her exploits around the office, out of the office gossip windmill. Maybe it just never got back to her because everyone knew Toni and Jada were close friends. Darien was not Toni's first office fling. For some reason Toni saw the work place as her own personal dating service. Jada tried to get her to come to church with her and David so she could meet a nice man there, but that didn't interest her. Toni was not raised in church and had not grown to appreciate its importance yet. Jada remained confident that one day Toni would. Until then, Jada would continue to invite Toni as often as possible and say a silent prayer at night, for her friend to find true love.

Toni kept her cell phone by her side for the rest of the day and night. She kept picking it up to make sure she had not missed any calls. Then she remembered the call she got just before she left to go meet Jada. The person didn't leave a message, so she had no idea who it was. Toni decided to write the number down before it got deleted out of her phone.

Chapter 5

Jada

At work the next day, I focused on getting to know this Darien person more. Of course, I had to do all of my detective work without Toni finding out about it, or I would get an earful. I also had to be careful about tipping anyone else off about their relationship. I knew he worked in accounting, but had no idea what he did, or who he worked for. The first thing I did was look him up in our address book. I was surprised to see that he was listed as a Manager of Accounting for our Eastern region. Hmm, I said to myself. This is a few steps up from the last guy. He was a mail clerk in the mailroom. Not that there is anything wrong with a guy being a mail clerk, but Toni is a Manager and needs to set her sights a little higher. Therefore, this guy already had one thing going for him. He was in management. I was further impressed to see that he had several direct reports and an assistant. I knew his direct supervisor but not well enough to get any useful information from him. I was going to have to use my ace in the hole, which was my girl Linda from Human Resources. Linda clearly should not be in HR because she could not keep a secret to save her soul. She was a nice girl but always gave out way too much information. I was going to have to be careful when I called her to inquire.

I could not let on that I needed to know because of my friend Toni being in a relationship with him.

I had some outstanding paperwork for a new hire, so I needed to contact HR anyway. I decided to call Linda and ask about the paperwork, and then I would engage her in some chitchat about office gossip to see if she knew anything first. If the word was out on the street about Toni's lunchtime activities, Linda would know it. I dialed Linda's number and the phone barely rang. It sounded like she snatched the phone off its cradle as if she was waiting for my call or something.

"HR, Linda speaking," she panted into the phone.

"Hi Linda," I said. "How are you today?"

"I'm good Jada," she said.

"Sorry I just ran back into my office when the phone rang". Whispering she said, "Did you hear about..." I cringed as I braced myself to hear Toni's name, but was pleasantly surprised when she continued, "Jonathan, in IT?"

"No," I said. "What happened?"

"He got walked out on Friday. Rumor is, he was video chatting on some porn website in his office."

I gasped and said, "You cannot be serious Linda. How could someone be so stupid?"

"I don't know Jada, but this kind of thing happens all the time."

"Wow," I said, shaking my head.

"What else has been going on around here Linda? You seem to always have the latest and greatest information."

"It's been pretty quiet the past few weeks. Nothing juicy, just the normal office hook ups and break ups," she answered.

I saw this as my opportunity to probe deeper to see if there was anything circulating about my girl Toni.

"Have you heard any new gossip from the Harrisburg office?" I asked. Linda worked out of our Pittsburgh office but she knew more about the goings on in Harrisburg than I did most days. I continued, "I heard a lot of the single ladies are fawning over the new guy in accounting."

"Oh Darien," she giggled. "He's not really new. He worked out of this office as an intern during college and then came on full time out of college. He recently transferred to the Harrisburg office to be closer to his family."

"Oh," I said, "so he's married with children?"

"No" she said, "He is from Harrisburg and his mother and younger sister are still there. When he put in his request for transfer he just said he needed to be closer to his family," Linda said.

"So how do you know he's not married?" I asked.

I was getting a vibe from her that she really knew more about him than she was letting on.

"Well," she said, "actually I dated him briefly while he was an intern and still in college."

She sounded indifferent about it.

"Oh I see. So it didn't work out with you two, huh?"

"No, we were both just feeling each other out. Neither one of us wanted a serious relationship. In fact I know Darien is not interested in settling down anytime soon."

"Really?" I asked.

"Yep," Linda said in a matter of fact voice, "He's one of those guys who say they will always be single. Based on what I know I believe that will be the case. He's got this crazy thirty day sex test thing that he likes to put women through."

"Whoa," I said. "Linda this is getting a little too personal for me."

She laughed and said, "Sorry I always do that, give too much information. So, anyway, I know you didn't call me to talk about Darien so what's up?"

I spent the next few minutes talking about legitimate HR stuff with Linda but my mission had been accomplished. I had some good information about Darien. The problem is what would I do with that information? Almost on cue, as soon as I hung up the phone with Linda, Toni walked into my office. She plopped herself down in one of my visitor chairs.

"Well no word from Darien since he left my house yesterday. It has been almost 24 hours and no phone call. That's not a good sign."

Here we go again, I thought to myself, and said "Toni. How did you leave things with him yesterday when he left?"

She stood up started pacing and said, "I don't know. We were standing by the door and he was acting like he didn't know what to say so, I said something like I had a good time and would like to do this again sometime and call me."

"Ok" I said, "So it's only been 24 hours so he hasn't had time to get hungry again to ask you out to eat."

Toni was not amused. She was really upset by his lack of communication. See this was her problem. She was very inpatient and in my opinion unrealistic of her expectations of men in general.

"Toni," I said. "It's not even lunchtime yet. Why don't you give him sometime to collect his thoughts before you jump to conclusions about what's on his mind?"

"I'm trying," she said and she sat back down and put her head down on her lap.

"Why don't you give him until the end of the week to reach out to you before you get all worked up about it?"

She jumped up and said, "The end of the week, are you kidding me? I won't survive that long." She was very melodramatic

"Yes you will Toni. You know why?"

"Why?" she asked

"You will be fine because we've a very busy work week and you need to be focused on that not Darien. You had a great date the other night right?"

"Yes," she answered.

"Well based on what you described to me yesterday you should still be basking in the after glow for another day or two anyway."

That made her blush a little and she said, "Yes I guess you're right. Ok I will give him until Wednesday."

"What about Thursday?" I asked.

"Okay," she agreed, "but Thursday morning."

"Deal," I said and reached across my desk to shake her hand.

She laughed and bounced out of my office. I sighed to myself and thought about how I was going to break the news to Toni about the new love of her life. This was not going to be good at all.

Vince

Sitting in my home office planning my day, thinking about the fact that I really needed to make something happen soon, or I was going to have to get a real job. I was making a little bit of money managing a few local bands and aspiring singers. Also, I had a few studio gigs writing jingles for commercials, but I really wanted to write and produce music, full time. I knew Harrisburg was not the best place for this but this was home and it was close to Philadelphia and New York. I was not giving up, but I needed to have a solid plan B soon. Especially since Gina and I seem to be hitting it off and at some point, she is going to want more from our relationship. I'm not in a position to propose, or anything long-term commitment-wise until my future is a lot more secure than it is today.

It occurred to me early this morning that I had not heard from Darien after his non-date with Toni. I was surprised because I know he had big plans for a serious freak fest and would usually be chomping at the bit to call me to share all the sordid details with me. Gina had not left for work yet, so I would wait until she was gone to give him a call. I wanted to hear all the details and didn't need to hear her mouth about my immature disgusting friend, Darien. Gina didn't really like him all that much, and I guess I could understand why. She didn't want me picking up any of his bad habits.

As soon as I heard Gina's car pull off, I was dialing Darien's cell. It went straight to his voice mail, which meant he was in a meeting or something, and could not be disturbed. I left him a message to give me a call as soon as possible. I made it sound urgent and didn't let on that I wanted to hear about his date with Toni.

Darien

When I arrived at the office on Monday morning, my boss was waiting for me, which was not a good sign at all. As I had feared, one of our newest acquisitions was not going so well. My boss let me know that we recently discovered major problems with their financial reporting and we had to conduct a full audit, and this had to be completed in the next 30 days. This meant I was going to be spending a lot of time out of town, on-site working with the accountants. The good news was that the office was in Miami, Florida; not like the last one, which was in North Dakota. Time was of the essence, so my assistant had already made my travel arrangements and I was scheduled to leave later today. As soon as I was finished talking to my boss, I packed up my briefcase and laptop and headed back home to pack for my trip.

On my way home, I called my mom to let her know I would be leaving, and was not sure, when I would be back. My mom was a single mother and struggled to raise my younger sister, Joy. Joy was 16 and a handful. She is part of the reason I decided to move back home to help my mom out with her. Raising a teenager these days was tough and my mother was a little older than most parents raising a child her age. Joy's father was long gone and was absolutely no help. He is probably one of the reasons I really didn't want children, because I knew the kind of father I didn't want to be. I was not sure if I could be any different than he was right now. He liked the ladies and they unfortunately took a priority over his flesh and blood. My father was not really involved in my life either but I knew who he was and we did talk from time to time. He died while I was in

41

college. My mom met Joy's father after she and my dad decided it just was not going to work. They never married.

I promised my mom I would check on them every day while I was away and she assured me that they would be fine without me. She always teased me about how over protective I was with both she and Joy.

I was packed and at the airport by noon. My flight was at 1:15, so I had some time to check my messages. I picked up a voice message from Vince asking me to call right away. It sounded urgent, so I found a quiet place in the terminal and dialed his number. He answered on the first ring, as if he was sitting on top of the phone waiting for it to ring.

"Hello Darien," he said. "So what's with not calling me, and letting me know about your date with Toni man?"

I could not believe this is what the urgency was. I said, "Vince is this what you were calling me about man?"

He chuckled and said, "Yeah man, what else would I be calling about?"

I sucked my teeth and said, "I can't talk to you right now man. I'm at the airport. Ran into some problems with our newest acquisition and I'm headed to Florida for God only knows how long. Therefore, I'm going to have to call you later on to tell you about Toni. Okay?"

"Oh, ok man," Vince said. "I didn't know what was going on with you. That's cool. Hit me up when you get settled and have some time to fill me in on all of the details."

I laughed and said, "You know I will. I'll talk to you later man."

Chapter 6

Darien

My trip to Miami was uneventful. I made it to my hotel by 6 pm. I was glad that I didn't have to go straight to the office. I had some time to review everything and decide what my approach was going to be. I took some time on the plane to review the packet of sample reports my assistant had put together for me. For tonight, I was going to order room service, review everything in detail again, and jot down some notes for my meetings tomorrow. I also owed Vince a phone call and I had to check in with my mom. She always worried when I traveled, so I had to call and check in. I often wondered how old you have to be before you no longer have to check in with mom.

I settled into my room and made the call to my mom. She was excited to hear from me and let me know that everything was good back home with her and my sister. As I listened to my mom chitchat about the neighborhood gossip, I checked out the room service menu and decided on the steak salad.

"Ok mom," I said. "Well I've got to go, so I can order my dinner and start getting prepared for my meetings tomorrow."

"Ok babe," she responded.

"Be safe and let me know when you're coming home, okay?"

"Yes ma. I will be here for at least the rest of the week, but I will check in on you every few days. Also, call me on my cell phone if you need to. Love you much."

"I love you too, son."

I called and ordered my dinner and then checked the time. It was only 6:30, but Vince should still be home alone. This would be a perfect time to call him to talk before Gina got home. I dialed his number and he answered on the third ring.

"Hey man," he said. "So you made it to Miami safely?"

"Yeah man. I'm here and getting settled and ready for my meetings tomorrow. Gina isn't home is she?"

"No, not yet. She is working late tonight."

"Ok good. I wanted a chance to talk to you before she got home."

"Yeah man. You have been holding out on the details of your date with Toni. So what happened?" he asked.

"Well it was actually pretty nice. I mean things didn't go *exactly* as I planned, but we both had a great time and she's a real nice girl."

"So what *exactly* does that mean that things didn't go according to your plan? You didn't end up in bed with her?"

"Or course we ended up in bed man. I didn't say it was a disaster. I just didn't get to use all of my toys like I wanted to."

Laughing, Vince said, "Man you're a trip. Please tell me you didn't take your kinky sex toys over to that girl's house."

"Actually I did" I said then continued "but she never knew anything about it. After dinner when we got back to her place, she had her room set up with candles and soft music. That wasn't the right setting for what I had planned."

"So how did you get out of there man? I know you were not feeling the candles and soft music routine." I was surprised at his reaction. He really thought I bailed on her because of the mood she was trying to set.

"Vince, why do you think I wouldn't be down with that?"

"Well, Darien it's just that all you kept telling me is how freaky she was and all you wanted to do was sex her up; not have a relationship with her."

"Boy, you're sure hard on a brother. You act like I've never had a relationship before."

"Well," he said, "you really haven't had a relationship."

"Vince you're tripping. I've had some relationships, maybe not on complete lockdown like you, but I'm capable of being in a relationship with a woman."

As I was arguing about my ability to have a relationship with a woman, I was thinking back to the last time I actually did have one, and was having a hard time thinking of one. Damn maybe Vince was right.

Vince interrupted my thoughts and said, "So you didn't leave. You stayed and kept your toys in your bag and had a nice time, is what You're telling me?"

"Yes," I answered. "I actually stayed the night and was served breakfast in bed," I said bragging.

There was dead silence on the phone for a minute. I actually took the phone from my ear to look to make sure the call had not dropped. Then all of a sudden, I heard Vince laughing hysterically into the phone.

"Man what are you laughing about so hard?" I asked. He continued laughing and then said faintly, "you."

"Me? Why?" I asked.

Vince continued, "You mean to tell me after all that plotting and planning, you slept with her at her place with candles and soft music playing in the background? You spend the entire night and you let her serve you breakfast in bed? Sounds like she had some plotting and planning of her own and she won."

He was still laughing hysterically and I was thinking about everything he said. Did Toni really set me up? No it all seemed so innocent. Why was I letting Vince get in my head like this?

"Look Vince, I know what I said was going to happen, but it didn't turn out that way. I had a good time and so did Toni. Why can't we just leave it at that?"

"We can" Vince answered then continued, "I'm just pleasantly surprised, so how did you leave things with her? When are you going out again? Have you talked to her since?"

He was sure asking a lot of questions.

I said, "We left it that we would be in touch with each other when we wanted to spend time together again."

Vince then asked, "So have you talked to her since Sunday morning?"

"No and it's only Monday night," I said quickly.

"I was going to email her today, but when I got to the office I found out about this emergency trip."

Actually, I do not have her number I thought to myself then continued, "We hooked up at the office and we've always corresponded via email or through IM at work. I've her cell number written down in my office, but not with me."

Vince said, "All I can tell you is that girl is waiting for your call man and if you don't call soon it's going to be a problem."

There was a knock on my door, which meant my room service had arrived.

"Vince man, my dinner is here so I'm going to have to go man. I will be in touch with you later in the week."

"Alright man. I'll talk to you later." he said.

I was not sure what to think about Vince's reaction to how things turned out. I did have a good time, and I did intend on calling Toni again. Now that I was out of town and I knew the next month or so was going to be hectic, I was not sure how to handle this situation. I thought about all of this while I ate my salad, which was excellent. I considered calling Vince back to get advice on how to proceed, but thought better of it. He had already given me his opinion and I really was not in the mood to hear anymore, at least not tonight. I decided I would deal with this Toni thing later because I really needed to focus on preparing for my meetings the next day.

Toni

Journal Entry
Monday

   It has been one day since we last saw each other, or talked. I want to write so much, but I'm afraid. I'm afraid that I will look back on my thoughts later and feel silly or ashamed of how I felt. I feel liberated, refreshed. Today was just as stressful as all my days are at work but today I was not as affected by it. My thoughts of our time together bring me a sense of peace. I was a little bummed that I didn't see you or hear from you today. All day long, I was fighting the urge to stop by your office, or call you. I do not want to seem too eager. What is funny is that if you called me right now and asked to come over, or wanted me to come to your place I would be there in two seconds flat. See here I go being over zealous. I have to calm down and be patient. I've got to work on patience. That's just something I do not have a lot of. I'm hoping to hear from you soon. I want to know what is next for us.

Darien

   I finished reviewing all of the sample reports and made my notes for my meetings tomorrow by about 10 pm. I turned on the TV and flipped through the channels. In the back of my mind, I was thinking about how I was going to contact Toni. I could always email her but I really wanted to talk to her. Something about her voice, I wanted to hear it. I decided once I got to the office tomorrow I would email her, get her cell again and call her later in the evening.

Chapter 7

Darien

The next morning I arrived at the office early, 7 am. My first meeting was at eight and I wanted to get logged in, so I could email Toni. Apparently, no one gets in until at least 8 am around here. I basically sat in the lobby until 7:45 waiting for someone to sign me in. I decided immediately to visit on site Human Resources to request my own badge, so I can come and go as I pleased in this building. I could not afford to waste time waiting for people to let me in. This minor set back meant my contact with Toni was going to have to be later than I had planned.

After my first meeting started shortly after eight, I was in an endless series of meetings until almost 7 pm. I barely had a minute to eat the sandwich one of the assistants brought me around 2:30, when I became so malnourished I thought I might pass out. I had not had a chance to check emails or voice mails all day long. My boss was right. This plan was a mess. Their financial reporting packages were very complex and the data to compile the reports came from a variety of sources. This was going to make the audit much more difficult, but my team had come up with a solid plan of attack. I felt comfortable with our approach and I felt we had the right people assigned and we would be able to accomplish the goal but it was going to take some extra night and weekend hours. We set up daily status meetings and decided that on Thursdays, we would decide if those of us from other locations could travel back home for the weekend on Friday or not.

I didn't get a chance to email Toni today and at this point, I was tired and wanted to head back to my room. I decided I would try to log on from the hotel to check my messages and to send one to Toni. At least she would get it first thing tomorrow.

Toni

Well another day has passed with no Darien sighting at the office, no email, and no phone call. I was starting to get very anxious. Jada was very busy today; her office door was closed all day long so, I didn't have a chance to complain to her about not hearing from Darien. I checked a few times to see if he was logged into the instant messenger application and he was not so I'm not even sure he was at work today at all. Suddenly, I became overcome with the feeling that something terrible had happened to him. I mean I had not seen or heard from him since he left my house on Sunday morning. What if he was in a terrible accident or something? I would never know. I decided that had to be it. He was laid up in the hospital somewhere, and I was getting upset because he had not called me. I thought about calling Jada to review my theory with her but it was late, and I knew she would be upset because we agreed I would wait until Thursday morning to contact him.

Journal Entry
Tuesday

As each day passes my thoughts of you and desire for you increase. When I close my eyes, I can drift back in time and feel your touch and I imagine I hear your voice. Oh how I wish I could hear your voice. I've let you get under my skin, and I feel very vulnerable because I know I'm in a position to get hurt. You told me when we first met, you were not looking for a relationship, and I agreed to your terms. I never expected you to be such a nice guy. I really want to call you but I promised Jada I would wait until Thursday.

In the middle of my entry, I checked the clock and it was only 10:15 pm.

It's not too late to call, I thought to myself. I grabbed my phone and dialed the number. The phone rang four times. I was just about to disconnect the call when he picked up and answered with a simple, "Hello."

"Hi Darien," I said. "This is Toni."

"Well hello, Ms. Toni," he said and I felt like he was smiling through the phone. "I was just thinking about you."

"Really?" I said. "That's funny because you didn't call me I called you," I said with a hint of sarcasm.

"About that," he started, "I wanted to call you but I got sent out of town on business suddenly yesterday morning. I didn't have your cell number on me. I've been in meetings all day long and have not had a minute to log in to send you an email."

Trying to sound cool, I said "Darien its okay. I was just concerned because I had not heard from you since you left my house on Sunday, and I had not seen you around the office either. I thought maybe something had happened to you and I just wanted to check on you."

"Oh I see, well as you can hear, I'm doing okay. Just been busy with work and I will be busy for the next few weeks. I'm in Miami right now and am not sure, when I'm coming home. Hopefully this weekend, but not sure I really want to fly all the way back home just for the weekend when the only thing waiting for me there is my empty bed and my fish."

Trying to sound very nonchalant, I said, "Yes I can understand that."

We talked for another few minutes. Then I said, "Darien it's getting late so I need to go. Did you save my number in your phone?"

"Yes I did."

"Okay so call me when you can."

"I will Toni, I promise."

Journal Entry
Tuesday continued…

I broke down and called you and even though Jada is going to have some choice words for me, I'm glad I did. I really enjoyed talking to you. Our conversation left me wanting more. I'm trying to put my finger on what it's about you that intrigues me the most. I think it's a combination of a number of things. First of all, I like your confidence. You carry yourself like you know exactly who you are and what you want. That's a real turn on. In addition, you try to act like you're a player and women do not mean that much to you, but I can tell that you really like women. The way you talked about your mom and little sister I can tell you really like women. I mean most straight men like women. They love us and want to make love to us, but they do not really like us. I can tell you do. It's the way you listen that makes the difference. Women like to be heard more than anything else. I could write so much more but am very tired, so am closing for now. I'm looking forward to hearing from you tomorrow.

I placed my journal back in its hiding place, put my cell phone on the charger, and prepared to turn in for the night. As soon as I turned the light off my cell phone rang. I looked at the clock and it said 11:00 pm. *Who is calling me this time at night?* I thought to myself. I reached over to grab my phone off the charger to look at the number. It was an unfamiliar out of town number. I think the same one from the other day. *Who is this who keeps calling me?* I thought. I considered letting it go to voice mail again but I had a feeling I needed to take this call so I answered, "Hello".

"Hey baby," was the response on the other end of the phone. I could not believe my ears. I looked around my room and pinched myself to make sure I was really awake and I had not fallen asleep and this was a sick dream.

I said, "Hello"

Again and the voice responded with a chuckle, "Hey baby, it's Benjamin. I know you recognize my voice."

Okay so this time I did drop the phone and let out a little squeal. I sat on my bed staring at my phone as it lay on the floor beside my bed. I've no idea how long I just sat there before I knelt down to retrieve my phone. Once I did, I tentatively placed it back to my ear and listened to see if he

53

was still there. I could hear him breathing into the phone. After another minute or so of listening to him breathe, I said, "Benjamin, why are you calling me?"

He responded "I'm calling you because I missed you and I was thinking about you baby."

"Please stop calling me *baby!*" I screamed into the phone. I closed my eyes in an attempt to block the painful memories that were coming back. Shaking my head, I said, "Benjamin I can't do this right now. I do not know why you called me now but I cannot talk to you right now. Not like this."

I heard a heavy sigh on the other end of the phone and then he said, "Okay listen. I meant what I said. I miss you and I've been thinking about you. Also I'm going to be in town this coming weekend so, I wanted to know if we can meet for lunch or dinner, so we can talk."

I still could not believe this was happening and I didn't want to commit to anything without consulting with Jada, so I responded "Um I need some time to think about it Benjamin. Your call kind of caught me off guard. Can I get back to you later about lunch?"

Sounding irritated, he said, "sure no problem. I will call you back on Friday. Is that enough time for you to make up your mind?"

"Yes," I said, "that would be perfect."

"Ok great, Toni I know I've a lot of explaining to do and I will, I promise. Just give me a chance, okay baby?"

Trying to hold back the tears that were pooling in my eyes, I said, "Benjamin I will talk to you when you call me on Friday. I've to go now. Good bye."

After I hung up the phone, I sat for what felt like hours just staring at my phone and replaying in my head the brief conversation. I tried to force myself not to remember my time with Benjamin. I referred to them as the Benjamin years. Jada and I sometimes joked about my life in segments. There was the BB or before Benjamin years, and then the AB, or after Benjamin years. Jada says I changed after Benjamin. She will never say if it was good or bad, she just says I'm different. Jada does not even know everything that happened between Benjamin and me. In fact, Benjamin didn't even know the real reason why I went to Chicago for our final semester. I was not sure I was ready to open up those wounds. I spent years in therapy trying to get over Benjamin, and the guilt I felt for decisions I made without consulting him. I had convinced myself that somehow, Benjamin had discovered the truth, and that's the reason why he disappeared on me into thin air. I thought about all the plans we had made. He was going to be drafted into the NBA. We would get married and I would stay home and raise our children. What a great plan that was until he got injured and was unable to play basketball anymore. I knew that basketball was a major part of his life, but I never imagined him losing his chance to play would make him turn his back on me like he did.

I returned my cell to the charger, turned off the light and tried to fall asleep. I didn't look at the clock, but I know I lay awake for hours remembering the Benjamin years. I wondered what Jada would say tomorrow when I told her about my phone call.

Chapter 8

Jada

I had just gotten out of bed and turned my cell phone on, when it rang. It was only 6 am and I looked to see who was calling me so early. It was Toni.

"Hey girl," I answered cheerfully.

"Jada," Toni started, "You're not going to believe what happened last night."

I rolled my eyes and I felt certain that a lengthy description of some major dramatic event was about to begin. Therefore, I responded, "Toni, I just woke up and have to get the kids up and ready. Can't this wait until we get to work or lunch maybe?"

There was a brief pause and then she said, "Benjamin called me."

Now I was hysterical "WHAT!!!" I screamed into the phone. "Are you serious?"

"Yes, I am Jada."

"Oh my God! How in the hell did he get your number Toni?" I asked.

Toni responded, "I have no idea Jada, but I'm a mess. Can you please come over here? There is no way I can go into work today."

I thought for a minute and said "Toni, I have to go into the office today, because I have a deadline, but I'm pretty sure I can get out of there early. Let me check with David to see if he can be here for the kids."

I heard sniffling on the other end of the phone and then Toni said, "Okay Jada. I understand just get here as soon as you can *please*."

After I hung up the phone, I walked into the bathroom where David was and just stared at him. He was getting ready for work. When he saw me he smiled and then he turned around and said, "What's wrong baby? You look like you saw a ghost."

I shook my head and said, "I think I did David. Did you know Benjamin was out?"

The look on his face said it all. He did know, but he had not told me.

"David, why didn't you warn me?" I said and I turned to walk out of the bathroom. David followed me and said, "Jada, I wanted to tell you, but I just couldn't find the best time. I knew you would be upset and concerned so I just didn't want to deal with it."

I was so mad. Tears were welling up in my eyes. "David please tell me you didn't give him Toni's number."

He was shaking his head no, "No Jada. You know I would never do that. What happened between Toni and Benjamin affected me just as much as it affected you. I would not want to go through all of that again. So did Toni tell you what Benjamin said to her?" David asked.

"No. She didn't give me any specifics. Just that he called and wants to see her. I guess he is supposed to be coming here this weekend."

"He said he is coming here?"

"Yes. Toni said he told her he would be here this weekend. David can't you try to get in touch with him and talk him out of coming here?"

"Jada, I will try to get in contact with his cousin to see if I can get a message to him, but you know Benjamin and I don't really talk anymore since the incident."

"I know David, but this is serious. Can you please try to get in contact with him as soon as possible?"

"Yes babe. I will do what I can to nip this in the bud."

I rushed to get the kids and myself ready; I wanted to hurry up and get to work. I needed to get everything done, so that I could head over to Toni's house, as soon as possible. I knew my girl was having a meltdown. Benjamin was the one who Toni thought she would marry and live happily ever after with. He broke her heart in the worse way possible. He vanished with no explanation at all. I knew Benjamin had gotten into some trouble at a college party and had gotten locked up. I didn't know all the details, but I knew that David had convinced me to keep it all from Toni. Benjamin didn't want Toni to know he was in jail. We concocted a story about him getting hurt real bad during a play off game and he was going to be unable to play ball. He sunk into a deep depression and asked not to be contacted by anyone. I was worried that Benjamin would spill the beans to Toni that I knew where he was all these years and didn't tell her. Toni had assumed he met someone else and ran off and got married. That's what they had always planned to do. At one point, she had convinced herself that he was dead since she no longer heard from him. She could not imagine him just disappearing into thin air like he did.

This situation with Benjamin is part of the reason why we came to live in Pennsylvania and didn't return to our

home town of Greenbelt, Maryland. There were too many of
Benjamin's family there, and Toni didn't need to find out
that he was locked up. She would have put her entire life on
hold to wait for him. Although I didn't know all the details
of what happened that night, I knew that she didn't need to
be associated with the likes of him. I had known Benjamin
for years and never imagined he would get himself caught
up into some serious mess like he did. He ended up being
convicted of rape and attempted murder of a young girl.
David's father, David Sr.'s law firm represented Benjamin,
but they were unable to get him acquitted of the charges.
Turns out that the girl was only sixteen and still in high
school but she attended a college frat party. Toni missed all
of the action since she was doing an internship in Chicago
during our final semester in college. It was easy to hide the
truth of Benjamin's whereabouts since she was not even in
the state at the time it happened, and she was away during
the trial. The four of us Toni, Benjamin, David, and I grew
up in the same general area in Maryland. We ended up in
high school together and then all decided to attend Penn
State together.

The boys were major basketball stars. Well, Benjamin
was a starter. David played, but was never as good as
Benjamin. He realized pretty quickly that he didn't have a
future as a player once he got to Penn State, rode the bench
for most of his first and second season, and decided to
become a trainer instead, so he could still be around the
game. He also had dreams of one day becoming a coach.
Toni and I were both business majors. The four of us were
very close and had planned our futures, or so we thought,
down to how many children and what city we would live in.
When I thought back to all those plans, and how different

everything had turned out for all of us, it made me a little sad. I would actually get angry at Benjamin for being so irresponsible and getting himself into trouble whenever I saw that sad look in Toni's eyes. She had a terrible time for first few years after he disappeared. Although she had gotten better and started dating other men, I always knew where her heart was. Darien actually was the first guy, in a long time that, I felt had really made her forget about Benjamin.

David

I could not wait to leave the house, so that I could call my father. I knew Benjamin was out of jail, but never in a million years did I think he would make contact with Toni. I thought he knew better than to do something crazy like that. In fact, I was surprised he would have contacted her first. I would have thought I would have been the first person he went after, if he was going to try to dredge up the past. Benjamin and I grew up together and were best friends all through school. We played basketball together in high school and college until we ran into an unfortunate situation during our final semester; that one night, changed many lives forever. Jada and I were expecting our first child and focused on graduating and starting our lives together. Benjamin and Toni were both hopeful that he would get selected for a team in the NBA draft. I needed to call my father and consult with him about getting in contact with Benjamin. My dad was less than thrilled about *the Benjamin situation* when I called him. He told me to come to his office right away, so that we could discuss what our next move was going to be. It would take me at least an hour and a half to get to his office, which was in Baltimore, but this was important, so I called into my office to let my assistant know I needed to take a personal day and I started down to Baltimore.

When I arrived at my father's office, he was expecting me. His assistant told me to go right in. I walked into his office and closed the door behind me. David Sr. was pacing behind his desk looking out of the window, which faced the harbor. I loved my father's office and the view. He turned to me with worry in his eyes and said, "So, junior what do you think Benjamin wants?"

I thought for a minute and said, "Dad it's probably as simple as he wants to explain to her what happened and why he just disappeared. You know they were really in love."

My father started pacing again and said, "yes, but we had a deal didn't we? My law firm got him the least amount of time behind bars in exchange for him never contacting any of the parties involved again."

It was my turn to start pacing around his office. "I know dad," I started, "but you know I was never comfortable with that arrangement. Benjamin and I were friends and he really loved Toni. He gave up his life to save mine. That's not something I'm proud of. I should have been the one in jail not him."

My father walked over to me and spun me around, "Junior, you know that we made the best decision for everyone involved at the time right?"

Shaking my head I said, "I'm not so sure dad. I have not been sure for a long time now. Every time I see Toni, and the pain she still suffers every day, I feel responsible for it."

My dad let out a sigh and said, "Junior, you really should have thought, about that before you got involved with that other girl at that party, and let things get way out of control."

I was trying hard not to get upset, but I felt all the emotions from seven years ago flooding back. Tears started to pool in my eyes and I said, "Dad I regret everything about that night, every day of my life, trust me."

My dad came over to me and gave me a hug and said, "Okay son, I know it was an unfortunate incident but we did what we thought was the best for everyone at the time. So now, what do you propose we do about Benjamin trying to contact Toni?"

I hesitated for a moment because I knew my father was not going to like my response, but it was the only answer at this point. "Dad I'm going to talk to Benjamin and hopefully get him to give me some time to talk to Jada first before he tells Toni everything. If Jada finds out the truth from anyone but me, it's going to be so much worse."

Thoughtfully my dad said, "I wish she never had to find out the truth. It's going to kill her and possibly your marriage you realize that, right son?"

I had considered that possibility, but hearing my father say it aloud made it seem more real to me, and a sudden shudder went down my spine. "Dad I'm going to have to face all of this one day anyway, so I would rather do it now. I hope Jada is able to forgive me. Speaking of Jada, I have to head back home because I have to be there for the kids when they get home. She is going to be with Toni."

"Okay son. Are you sure, you want to talk to him? I mean I could probably get someone to..."

I interrupted him before he could finish his thought. "No dad," I said. "Please don't try to fix this for me. I'm a grown man and I need to handle this situation now. You cannot keep cleaning up my mess for me."

My father looked like I had kicked him in the groin; he was in so much pain. He simply said, "Okay son keep me posted on your conversation with Benjamin and let me know how things go with Jada. I wish your mother were still here. She could talk to Jada for you."

I thought about my mother and how much I missed her, I also remembered how well she and Jada got along. They hit it off from the first day they met when I first brought her home to meet them in high school.

"You're right dad, mom would know exactly how to handle this situation. In fact, I wish she had been here when it all happened. Maybe we would have made different choices back then."

My father just looked out the window and said, "Maybe so."

My drive home seemed to take forever. I replayed the events of that night, seven years ago, over and over in my head. I tried to decide if I wanted to talk to Benjamin or Jada first. All I knew is that I needed more time, to get my thoughts together, to work through all of this. I was about twenty minutes from home when Jada called me to remind me about the kids. She was on her way over to Toni's house and would be home late. I told her I was almost home and would be able to take care of the kids. I was glad I had a few more hours before I had to face Jada again. I wanted to have time to get myself together, so she would not see how upset I was. Even though Benjamin was my best friend, and it would make sense for me to be emotional about him being in jail, at times I think she could tell there was much more to the story of that night than I was letting on.

I was torn. I wanted Benjamin to stay away so that none of this would come out, but I also missed my friend and thought about how good it could be having him back in my life. I always felt guilty about not once contacting him while he was in jail, but I was not supposed to have any contact with him. That was a part of the deal. I thought about which one of his family members I could contact to figure out how to get in contact with him. None of his relatives were aware that I was the one who should have been in jail, but I always felt like they resented the fact that he was in jail and I was as free as a bird when we were both at the same party. They all knew how close we were, so it would be safe to assume that I was somewhere nearby when everything went down. Little did they know I was right there because it was me, not Benjamin who had sex with the 16-year-old girl. Then she announced that she had set me up because she thought I was a future NBA player, I lost it and beat her within an inch of her life. I was not a violent person but on that night I had been drinking and earlier that night Jada and I had a fight about me going to the party in the first place. She was pregnant and wanted me to stay in with her. We had made it into the playoffs and I wanted to celebrate with the team. If I could have gone back and changed my decision about that night, I would have given my right arm to do so.

*   *   *   *   *

Benjamin heard the girl's cries for help and came into the room where we were. He actually pulled me off her and smacked me to bring me back to reality. Once I saw how badly beaten she was, I freaked out. Benjamin remained calm, called for help, and then called my father. By the time the police arrived, we had changed our stories, so that Benjamin was the one in the room with the girl and I came in and saved her. When I think back to how quickly, Benjamin made the decision to take the fall for me it made me feel like a complete ass. He had an entire career ahead of him and he gave it all up, because Jada was pregnant. I remember him telling me how important it is for a child to have both their parents around and he was not going to allow my child to be without a father because of one stupid decision. I protested to both Benjamin and my father, but I was out voted. Decision was made. Benjamin was the one. My father assured both of us that he would do a minimal amount of time if anytime at all.

My father was a powerful attorney and had friends in high places and he had connections. He was able to keep the press at bay and we were able to avoid a trial all together. Benjamin pleaded guilty in exchange for a lesser sentence and he was forbidden from contacting anyone that was involved, which included the girl and me. Benjamin's pride was on our side and he decided he didn't want Toni to know the truth about where he was. With the help of some of my father's contacts in the media, we were able to concoct a story about him getting injured during a practice session for one of our big play off games. Toni, being in Chicago, made the cover up very easy. I just had to keep Jada in the dark. Jada could never know that it was me who was with that girl and not Benjamin. The news of me being unfaithful alone would kill her and our relationship.

YESTERDAY'S LIES

Terri D.

Chapter 9

Benjamin

I was on cloud nine but nervous at the same time. Hearing her voice after all these years I still felt the same way about her. She sounded so different though. She sounded hard and cold, but I guess that's to be expected after how everything went down. Toni was, and still is, the love of my life. We dated all through high school and in college. She was the one I knew I could marry one day after I became a famous basketball star because she knew me before I had anything, so I knew her love was true. When she left during our last semester for her internship, it was the hardest thing ever. Toni was optimistic. She said this was preparing us for the NBA. She would not be able to travel with me all the time once we had children so this was practice for that. I loved her positive outlook on life. We talked everyday while she was away until the night I was arrested.

The only person in the world I loved more than Toni was my boy David. My mother had passed away while we were in junior high school. My father was never around. I knew who he was but he didn't play an important role in my life. David's family knew me and kind of took me in, even though I had other family - aunts, and cousins. We were like brothers. When David got himself into some serious trouble, I had to take the fall for him. He had so much ahead of him. Jada was expecting their first child and even thought Toni and I were madly in love, we didn't have anything like Jada and David had. I always saw their love as the most pure thing I had ever experienced. They were both each other's first, which is probably why David went a little buck wild in college, especially after Jada got pregnant.

Truthfully, David Sr. first suggested that we change our stories and say I was the one with the girl instead of David Jr. He said, in so many words, that I owed it to them since they took me in and helped me with college. When my mother died, she left me with nothing but bills. My other family members didn't have a lot of money either. David's father, being an attorney with his own firm, obviously had money. I never realized the debt I would pay for their love and financial assistance over the years until I was being taken away in handcuffs and David was walking around free. Everyone at the party was so drunk that night it was easy to convince everyone, including me, that I was the one with the girl, not David.

I had to decide if I was going to contact David or not. I always wondered if he told Jada the truth or not. Probably not knowing David Sr, he probably put a special clause in the deal that forbids David Jr from telling the whole truth and nothing but the truth. I was going to call David to let him know that I would be in town this weekend to see if he wanted to see me. The first thing I did, when I got out, was track each of them down to see where they were and what they were doing. I found it a little ironic that they decided to settle down in Pennsylvania, since that's where I was in jail. I thought they would go as far away from me as possible.

I decided to call David to talk to him. I dialed the number and he answered on the third ring. When I heard his voice, conflicting emotions came over me. Joy. Anger. I hesitated long enough for him to say hello twice.

"Hello David," I said into the phone.

He paused. Then exhaled and said, "I was wondering when you would get around to calling me. I heard you contacted Toni."

"David you know how I felt, I mean how I feel about Toni, so why wouldn't I call her as soon as I could?"

David sighed, "I don't know man. I guess I thought that after all this time you would have moved on."

That was ridiculous, I thought, and then said, "David I was in jail, man, not away on an extended vacation or a business trip. How would I've moved on, while I was in jail?"

David laughed nervously and said, "Yeah I guess you're right about that. So, how are you man?"

"I'm doing okay considering. I'm looking forward to trying to put all of this behind me and get on with my life. I'm hoping I can talk Toni into giving me another chance. How has she been? You and Jada have been keeping an eye on her for me right. She seemed really freaked out when I called her last night. You did explain to her what happened right?"

David

I needed to be honest with Benjamin about everything with Toni, but I really didn't want to do this over the phone.

I wanted to explain to him that Jada didn't know the truth. It was me, not him, and how that news would obviously have an impact on my relationship. Toni never got any of the letters he gave me to give to her, before he was officially sentenced and, sent away to serve his time. I do not know why, but I just felt it was better for her not to know anything. All she knew is that he had suffered a serious injury during practice for the play-off game and was no longer being considered for the NBA draft. When Jada and I delivered that news to her, she was devastated and wanted to go to Benjamin immediately. We explained to her that he was taking the news really hard and asked not to be contacted until he had time to deal with everything. At first, Toni would ask about him every day. Had we heard from him? Did we know where he was? After a year, she didn't ask anymore. None of us did. It was as if Benjamin never existed. Fortunately, Toni's internship in Chicago landed her a nice job working for the same company in their Harrisburg, PA office. She was the first to relocate their after college. Jada and I decided to join her, as we did our research, and it seemed like a really nice place to raise children. We were both able to find jobs, and within six months, we joined Toni in Harrisburg.

"Benjamin," I said. "I think it would be best for us to sit down and talk about everything face to face. Jada mentioned that you told Toni you were coming to town this weekend."

"Yes. I want to see Toni and I made plans to come this weekend."

I thought for a minute then asked, "Would it be possible for you to come a day earlier to see me first? I would like to sit down with you to talk to you about what has been going on for the past seven years. That way you will be more prepared for your meeting with her. How does that sound?"

"I would like that very much," Benjamin said. "I would love to see you and Jada and your kids. You have two now, right?"

I swallowed hard and then said, "Um, yes, we have two children, a boy, and a girl. Listen, Benjamin. You and I need to talk first before you can even see Jada."

Benjamin was not a dummy, so he quickly realized that neither Jada nor Toni were in on the real deal. "David, I cannot believe you have let this go on for over seven years and not told even your wife the truth."

He was right and I knew it, but I needed to remain calm and keep him calm, so I could get a handle on this situation.

"Benjamin, man please. Can you and I just sit down and talk face to face about all of this?"

There was a very long pause and then he finally, answered and said, "David I will meet you Friday at noon. You pick the place, call me in the morning, and tell me where to meet you."

All I could say was, "Thanks man. I will call you in the morning." Then I hung up the phone.

I walked around in a daze for the rest of the night. I kept trying to come up with a good excuse to give Benjamin for why I left my wife, and his girlfriend, in the dark all these years, while he sat in jail for something I had done. He was the best friend I had in the entire world and I had turned my back on him when he needed me the most. I was determined to make everything right between him and Toni. I knew that in the process, I risked losing Jada, but I was hopeful that the life we had built had a strong enough foundation to withstand this blow.

Darien

I checked several times throughout the day for Toni online in IM, but she was not logged in. I finally called her work number and got her voice mail that said she was out of the office today. I tried her cell and it went straight to voice mail. I was a little concerned because I just spoke to her last night, and thought she was expecting to hear from me today, but maybe something came up. Work was still crazy so I had plenty to do to keep me busy. I wanted to talk to her to decide if I wanted to try to come home this weekend, or not. I wanted to see her while I was there. If I didn't get in touch with her by tomorrow, I was just going to plan on staying and working through the weekend.

Toni

By the time Jada arrived at my house, I was a complete mess. I had not eaten anything all day and had cried so much I didn't have any tears or tissue left in my house. As soon as I opened the door, I leapt into her arms and starting sobbing again. She just held me and said nothing for a long while. When she finally released me, she grabbed my hand and led me into my living room. We sat down on the sofa. I was crying but managed to say "Jada, why would Benjamin wait all this time and then call me out of the blue like this?"

Jada shook her head and said, "Toni, I have no idea. What did he say to you?"

I stood up and starting pacing back and forth, while wiping my nose, and said, "He said he missed me and was thinking about me. He kept calling me baby just like we talked yesterday, or something. Doesn't he realize how long it has been since I've heard from him? I mean, who does that? Just stops calling you and never explains why and then waits seven years and calls like nothing ever happened?"

Jada said, "I don't know Toni. It seems very odd to me. I do not think you should see him. It has been too long and you have put all of that pain behind you. It's time for you to move on."

I sat back down next to Jada and said, "Jada do you understand how Benjamin leaving me like he did, affected me?"

Jada grabbed my hand again before she responded and said, "Toni, of course I know, I was there remember through it all."

I shook my head and said, "No Jada you were not there through it all. There are things you don't know Jada and those things are the reason why I must see Benjamin."

Jada

Toni was worse off than I thought she would be. I've seen her a mess before, but this was really bad. The worse part about it was that I was a part of the reason that she felt

75

the way she did. I mean, I knew where Benjamin had been all these years, but I had not told her. What kind of friend did that make me? I was torn right now. Should I come clean and tell her what I know, or wait to see what happens when she talks to Benjamin? Actually, I was hopeful that David would be able to convince Benjamin to stay away, and let us all move on with our lives.

When I saw what a mess Toni was, I felt like she deserved some answers. I was not going to tell her anything right now. She was still too much in shock from his initial phone call. I also wanted to give David some time to contact Benjamin and hopefully we could put all of this behind us without Toni finding out everything. I stayed with Toni for several hours. I convinced her to eat something and take a shower. While she showered, I wondered about what she meant about there being things I didn't know. After her shower, she looked much better and said she would be fine. She wanted to spend some time writing in her journal, so she told me I could leave and go home.

Toni

Journal Entry
Wednesday

It's amazing how much a person's life can change in just 24 hours. Yesterday, I was writing about how wonderful Darien is. Today I'm in such a different place. I hardly know where to begin. I spent most of my day crying and trying to forget the memories that were forcing themselves into my conscious and subconscious thoughts. Jada came over and spent the afternoon and most of the evening with me. Jada is convinced that I should not meet with Benjamin. She said it has been over seven years and I had put all of that behind me. Meeting with him now, will just re open all of those wounds. Jada does not understand that the wounds never closed. There has not been a day in the past seven years that I've not thought about Benjamin, at least once at some point. I've always wondered what happened to him, and to us. I always thought about all of the what if's that never were. Jada thinks she knows what is best for me, but she is wrong. I do need to see Benjamin and talk to him. I need to give him time to explain himself and I need to get a few things off my chest also. My decision was made. I was going to call him back tomorrow and let him know that I was going to meet with him. It had to be lunch, not dinner, and we could meet on Saturday. I would need a few days to get my courage up to tell him things I had kept buried deep inside of me all of these years.

The next morning I was feeling a little queasy, probably because I didn't eat until late last night, and decided to call into work and take the rest of the week off. I was going to need some time to get my thoughts together about my meeting with Benjamin. I spent the better part of the morning thinking about what to say when I called him to arrange the meeting. I made a quick call to Jada to let her know I was okay but would not be in the office this week. She sounded concerned and said she would check in on me later.

Benjamin

After my talk with David, I knew that I needed to get to him soon, because he had a lot of explaining to do. I was getting ready to pick up the phone to call him to see if we could meet later today, when my phone rang. I didn't recognize the number, but it was local. I answered the phone, "Hello."

"Hello, Benjamin, this is David Sr."

I should have expected this phone call but it did take me a little off guard. "Um, hello sir." Even thought I should be very angry and ready to lash out at him, I still had the utmost respect for David Sr.

He continued, "Benjamin, I would like to meet with you today, to discuss your intentions."

"My intentions?" I asked.

He answered, "Yes, I understand that you have been in contact with Toni, and my son."

"Yes, sir, that's correct. Is that a problem?"

He cleared his throat and then responded, "yes actually it is. Our deal was no contact."

"Yes, sir, that's correct, however, it was no contact during my time in jail. There was no stipulation about contact after my release. I had another attorney review the agreement, before I contacted Toni."

David Sr.

Maybe I had underestimated Benjamin. There was a glitch in the written agreement. An error on the part of my paralegal, it was supposed to be no contact during incarceration, or after his release, but the *after release* part was left out. He was right, there was nothing legally I could do to stop him from contacting any of the involved parties, but I had to do something to help my son save his marriage.

"Benjamin, would you please just come to my office, so that the two of us can talk?"

Benjamin thought for a minute and finally responded, "Sure, what time do you want me to be there sir?"

I let out a sigh of relief and asked, "how about noon?"

Benjamin responded, "Yes I will be there."

I wanted to convince Benjamin not to talk to Toni, but knew it was going to be difficult. Junior was right; Benjamin really loved Toni and keeping him away from her now, was going to be next to impossible. The best I could hope for was that he would agree to not letting Jada in on the truth about him taking the fall for David. I knew how Benjamin had felt about Junior before all of this happened. I hoped that his commitment to David Jr. would still be a driving force in his decision now. I nervously awaited his arrival.

Darien

I checked IM, again, and still no sign of Toni. Called her work number and my call went directly to her voice mail. Just as I was about to call her cell, my phone rang. I

79

checked the caller id and it was Vince calling. I answered, "Hey what's up man?"

Vince responded, yawning, "Oh nothing really man. Was just checking in to see if you decided if you were coming home this weekend, or not? Gina will be away, so I'll be looking for something to do."

I sighed and said, "I'm not sure yet. I'm waiting to get in touch with Toni again before I make my decision."

"Oh, so you finally got in touch with her then?" Vince asked.

"Actually she called me, the other night."

Vince laughed and said, "I told you man, she is going to turn into one of those stalker - chicks you seem to attract."

I was instantly irritated by his comment about Toni being a stalker. I didn't know why it bothered me so much, so I let it go and simply said, "She's a really nice girl and I enjoy her company. Can't we just leave it at that?"

Vince chuckled and said, "Sure we can leave it there man. Just sounds like maybe you're getting a little soft or something. I cannot remember the last time you talked about the same girl, on two separate days, and you said she was nice; last I knew, she was a freak."

I wanted to argue but he was right. I did feel a little different about Toni since our dinner date, but I was not going to admit that to him. Not right now. I needed some more time to figure out why I was so bothered by his comments and why she was constantly on my mind.

"Well Vince, "It doesn't look like I will be coming home this weekend, so you're going to have to find someone else to hang out with since Gina is going away."

Vince replied, "Okay man, well I guess I'll just work on my music this weekend then. I've some ideas for some songs in my head."

Just then, I thought about Toni's voice when I heard her singing the other morning and I said, "Hey Vince, I forgot to mention that Toni has an awesome voice."

He laughed and said, "Exactly when did you hear this wonderful voice? Was this when she was singing in the shower, or what man?"

"No actually it was while she was in the kitchen cooking a brother breakfast." The memory of that breakfast brought a smile to my face.

Vince said, "Oh yes, the breakfast in bed trick she pulled on you."

"Trick or no trick man, she can throw down in the kitchen, and the bedroom, so a brother was satisfied all the way around," I said with pride.

Toni might not be my girl officially, but for the moment, she was, and I knew she had one up on Vince's Gina because girlfriend could not boil water, to let him tell it. I knew I was hitting below the belt a bit with that last comment, but he deserved it with all the grief he has been giving me lately.

Vince sucked his teeth and said, "why, did you have to go there man? You know I'm working with Gina on her cooking skills."

Now I was laughing. "Whatever man, if you want to be with Gina, even though she can't cook, that's on you. All I'm saying is when I decide to get with a woman, she needs to know how to do it all."

Vince simply responded, "I hear you man, but remember you ain't never getting married."

After I got off the phone with Vince, I decided not to call Toni. I didn't want to travel all the way home just for one or two nights. Especially since I was not sure, I would get to see her anyway. I had a lot of work to do here, so I was just going to stay here for the weekend. I sent her an email letting her know I would not be in town this weekend, and would be in touch with her next week, or she could call me over the weekend if she got a chance.

Chapter 10

Benjamin

I was getting more and more nervous, the closer I got to David Sr.'s office. I had not seen him in years and even though I should be angry, or upset, I still felt a tremendous amount of respect for him. He had taken me in and helped raise me after my mother died. My cellmate, who I spilled my guts to while I was locked up, disagreed, but somehow I still felt that David Sr. had tried to do right by me during all of this. When I arrived at his office, I sat in my car for a while to gather my thoughts. I knew he was concerned about David, Jr and Jada. He really was not concerned about Toni. My main concern was Toni, and making her understand what happened. The problem was I could not tell her I was in jail for rape and attempted murder, and expect she would take me back. I had to let her know that it was not me, but David, Jr. who did those terrible things. This really was a no - win situation. Maybe I had not properly thought it all through before I jumped the gun and called Toni. Well I could not wait any longer; it was time to face David Sr. for the first time in over seven years.

David Sr.

I was pacing when he arrived. I turned to face him. I was surprised at how grown up he looked. I guess seven years in prison is a hard life, even for a young man. Benjamin walked over to me, gave me a nervous handshake, and said, "Hello sir, it's good to see you."

I mumbled, "It's good to see you also Benjamin and you're looking well. Go ahead and have a seat. Would you like something to drink?"

Benjamin sat down and responded, "No thank you, sir."

"Benjamin, please stop calling me sir. Just call me David, or senior okay?"

"Yes sir, I mean, David Sr."

I had been thinking all morning how to approach him about all of this. I decided to let him tell me what he wanted to happen and then I would determine my approach from there.

"So Benjamin, what are you plans now?"

He shifted in his chair and said, "What exactly do you mean sir, um I mean, David."

"Well I mean have you thought about what you plan to do for a living now that you're out?"

Maybe I could offer to help him get a good paying job in exchange for him leaving my son and his family alone, I thought to myself.

He started shaking his head and said, "No sir, I actually have not thought about that."

"Well Benjamin, maybe I might be able to assist you with finding a good job."

He stood up now, and starting pacing, then turned to me and said, "Look Sir, I mean David, if your offer is genuine, then yes I would love the help. If this is some ploy to keep me from contacting Toni, or David Jr. then I will have to say no thanks."

"Benjamin, exactly what do you expect to accomplish by bringing all of this up now?"

He sat back down and put his head in his hands. Then be brought them up to rest under his chin like he was praying. He turned to me and said, "Sir I love Toni more than life itself. I simply want a chance at the life we could have had if none of this had happened. Honestly, I had not thought through all the details of how this would play out, until now. I understand that in order for me to have a chance at happiness, I risk ruining what David and Jada have."

I started "yes that's true…"

He interrupted, "but I also know that what David and Jada had was ruined seven years ago, when he slept with that girl, and then beat her within an inch of her life. At the time, I felt like I was doing the noble thing saving David and Jada's relationship and preserving the family for their unborn child. Now I realize that I simply made matters worse by creating an impossible web of lies for everyone involved."

I could feel my blood pressure rising. I was getting very angry, but I knew Benjamin was right. This was an impossible situation that was caused by an act of stupidity on my son's part. I thought for a few minutes before I responded. Finally, I said, "Benjamin there is a way to have us both get what we want you know?"

He was shaking his head, no, but looked up at me and said, "How's that sir?"

"I believe if you talk to Toni, and explain the situation to her, she will keep the truth from Jada. She would not want to hurt Jada. Just like you didn't want to see David hurt back then."

"I'm not sure I could ask her to do that, sir," Benjamin responded.

"You won't have to. I think that you and David should both talk to Toni together. That way you can tell her where you have been; all these years, and then David can give his side of the story, and plead with her to keep Jada in the dark about the truth. Think about it. Jada already knows you were in jail, so would Toni. The only difference is that Toni would know it was David, not you, who did those things. Jada does not have to know. What do you think?"

Benjamin looked at me for a long while before he answered. I could tell he was weighing everything I had said before he answered. Finally, he said, "I think I'll take that drink now and let's call David Jr. to discuss this scenario with him."

David Jr.

I answered the phone on the first ring. I knew my father was meeting with Benjamin so I was expecting him to call when their meeting was over. "Hello, dad," I said. "So, what happened?"

"Actually son, Benjamin is still here. We have a proposal for you."

I could not wait to hear what scheme my father had cooked up this time. I was ready to be finished with all the lies, and just lay everything out on the table. I was surprised that my father had come up with something that Benjamin would agree to.

"So what's the plan dad?" I said.

I heard him moving the phone around, probably turning the speakerphone on and then he said, "I'll let Benjamin explain."

The next sound I heard was Benjamin's voice. He let out a heavy sigh and said, "David, I want to try to get back together with Toni. The only way I have a chance of doing that is to tell her the truth about where I've been for the past seven years. Well, if I tell her that I took the blame for your crime she might forgive me and take me back. The problem is getting her to keep the truth of your involvement from Jada."

"Yes," I said, "that will be the hard part. That's why I just want a chance to tell Jada myself."

Benjamin said, "But wait David, what if we talk to Toni and tell her the truth, but ask her not to tell Jada that it was you, not me?"

I actually had not even considered this as an option. I just assumed Toni knowing the truth, meant that Jada would know. The reality is that Jada has kept Benjamin's whereabouts from Toni all this time, so why was it so hard to imagine that Toni would do the same.

"Benjamin, you and dad might be onto something, but I have to think about it some, more and we all have to prepare for Toni not agreeing to withhold the truth from Jada once we let her in on it."

We continued to talk for a few more minutes and ultimately decided that Benjamin and I would meet with Toni together, but we decided that we were going to postpone the meeting to give us some more time to come up with a plan B, in case Toni would not agree to our terms. We also wanted to give my father some time to make good on his promise to help Benjamin find a job. Benjamin felt very strongly that he wanted to come to the table with a solid plan for him and Toni to get together again.

Benjamin

I felt strangely relieved after leaving David Sr.'s office. I felt like we might have found a way to make everyone happy. The only problem is that I really wanted to see Toni now, and David Sr. asked that I delay my trip to Harrisburg for a few weeks to give him some time to work with me to find me a job. David Jr. also wanted some additional time to work on what his plan would be if Toni didn't agree to keep Jada out of all of this. Now I had to come up with an excuse to tell Toni why my plans had changed for this coming weekend. I decided to get that phone call out of the way immediately. The longer I waited the worse it would be, I'm sure. I dialed Toni's number as I drove towards my cousin's house. As soon as she answered, I regretted agreeing to wait a few weeks to visit her.

"Hello there, baby," I said.

Toni responded like she had previously, "Benjamin please stop calling me baby."

"Okay Toni. I will try not to call you baby."

"Thanks," she said dryly.

"So, I was calling to let you know that something has come up, and I'm not going to be able to come up to see you this weekend, after all."

"WHAT!!!" she screamed into the phone. I was afraid of this reaction. "Benjamin, how in the hell do you just pop up and call me out of the blue after seven years, calling me baby? Get me all hyped about seeing you, so you can explain where the hell you have been for most of the last decade, and then you call me back to say *oh sorry I was just playing*. What the hell is wrong with you? Do you like playing with my emotions or something?"

I knew she was crying. This hurt my heart, but a deal was a deal, and I had to make good on this one. In the end, it would be better for us anyway.

"Toni, I'm very sorry, but something very important has come up, and I promise you: I will be in touch in the next few weeks to make arrangements to come and see you."

The last thing I heard was, "whatever Benjamin," and then the phone went dead.

David Jr.

I was very excited about the arrangement my father was able to get Benjamin to agree to. If nothing else, I had a little more time to figure out how to break the news to Jada, in case Toni would not go along with our scheme. After Benjamin left, my father and I talked some more and between my father's contacts and mine, we were going to try to find him a job. That was a part of the deal also. I could not wait to tell Jada that I was able to talk Benjamin out of coming to town this weekend. She was going to be very happy about that, I'm sure.

Jada

I was sitting in my office working on my latest proposal, when my cell phone rang. I had kept it close to me all day in case Toni called. I looked at the caller ID and it was in fact, Toni. I answered the phone, "what's up girlie? How are you doing?" I heard sobbing and a lot of incoherent gibberish, then sniffling. I said, "Slow down Toni. What is going on?"

She took a deep breath and said, "Can you believe that Benjamin just called and cancelled on me?"

I sat back in my chair, looked up to the ceiling, and mouthed,' THANK GOD' and then said, "Toni, I'm so sorry to hear that, but maybe it's for the best. I mean maybe he will not call again and you can continue to move on with your life. Remember Darien? He's supposed to be the one."

Toni sighed heavily into the phone and said, "Jada you just don't understand. I thought you would, but you clearly do not get it. I need to see Benjamin. Not just because I want to know where the hell he has been for the past seven years, but because I have some things I need to tell him."

This was the second time Toni alluded to the fact that there was some drama in her life I didn't know about. "Girl, what are you talking about? I thought you and I were tight, and I knew everything there was to know about you."

To this she responded, "yes we are tight and you will always be my girl, but aren't there some things that you and David share that I don't know about?"

Well she was right. There were those sacred marriage things you kept with just your spouse, so I could not argue that point, but she and Benjamin were not married. "Yes, Toni" I said. "You're right. So, these things you need to tell Benjamin about, will you ever share them with me?"

I could not lie I was very curious about what it might be. There was something very mysterious about how Toni ended up in Chicago for our last semester, and then in

Harrisburg, after graduation. Toni hesitated for a moment; I could hear her moving the phone around before she responded.

"I'm not sure Jada. I need some time to process all of this before I decide what my next move will be."

"Okay Toni" I said, "but have you decided what you're going to do about Darien in the meantime?"

"I'm not sure, but he's away on business for the next few weeks, so I have some time to figure that out," she said. We ended our conversation promising to keep in touch over the next few days as she sorted out her feelings and decided if she was going to clue me in on her big secret or not.

Chapter 11

Toni

After Benjamin's call, the emotional rollercoaster started for me all over again. I was overwhelmed by feelings of abandonment like the ones I felt all those years ago. I sat around for hours reminiscing about the last year that Benjamin and I spent together. I had already decided prior to his phone call to cancel, to tell him the truth about my internship. Something that no one, not even Jada knew about.

Benjamin was a superstar basketball player in college. He was being pursued by several NBA teams and was a sure thing for the first round of the draft. Benjamin and I had plans. He wanted to play for the San Antonio Spurs and they were one of the teams who were seriously looking at him as their first pick. While he was breaking into the NBA, I would finish my education. We had discussed me continuing on to get my master's right away. Something I wanted because once he was established I wanted to start our family. Benjamin said we would talk about kids later. He wanted them, but wanted to make sure he was ready. He didn't have a good relationship with his father and he wanted to make sure he was ready, and could devote his time to his children before he had any.

When I found out, I was pregnant half-way through the fall semester, I could not tell him. I knew Benjamin and I knew he would want to give it all up, his dream basketball career, to marry me and raise our child. It's ironic because Jada found out she was expecting right around the same time. In fact, the very day I confirmed I was pregnant, Jada announced that she was expecting, and she and David were getting married right after graduation. David's dreams of a career as a player in the NBA were over by his sophomore year. He never got much playing time, and eventually decided he wanted to coach, instead of playing.

My decision to keep my pregnancy from Benjamin was in part because I knew how he would react, but I also was not sure he was the father. Unlike Jada and David, Benjamin and I had more of an on-again/off-again relationship at times, in college. We loved each other, but for some reason we were both still curious about what else might be out there. The summer before our senior year, Benjamin and I had a huge fight about a friend of mine; Mario from junior high school came over to visit me. Benjamin had a terrible jealous streak. We broke up for a few months and right at the beginning of the semester; I met a guy at a party one night, named Vinny. Vinny and I went out on a couple of dates, and on our final date, we slept together. A week or so later Benjamin and I reconciled, and about a month later, I discovered I was pregnant. The baby could have been either of theirs. Benjamin and I had just gotten back together, and I was not sure what his reaction would be to me being pregnant, but I was also not sure he was the father. After we slept together, and Benjamin and I reconciled, Vinny called me several times but I never returned his calls.

An opportunity came up for an internship in Chicago, and I jumped at the chance. I would be able to be away during the later part of my pregnancy and no one, not even Jada, would know. I decided against telling Jada, too, because of everything she and David had going on. I spent my last semester in Chicago, and had the baby right before graduation. My plan had not always been to put the baby up for adoption. I wanted some time to sort things out and see what happened with the draft for Benjamin. If he had not vanished on me, I thought I would be able to come clean about the baby, and we could make a decision on how to proceed with our relationship. After his injury and he was told he would never play again, I thought maybe I could keep the baby and we could get married and start our family right away. I waited for him for three months before I decided to put the baby up for adoption. I even tried unsuccessfully to get in touch with Vinny, but I was never able to locate him. I never even knew the sex of the baby. I didn't want to know. It would be too hard. Always looking at every little boy or girl and wondering if that was my child. It was still that way but not knowing the sex of the child somehow seemed easier for me.

I thought about how I had lost the love of my life, and my child, at the same time. Jada thought she knew the pain I was feeling, but she didn't. She had her baby, and her man, and I envied her for that. I could never bring myself to tell her the truth. I was ashamed of my irresponsible behavior and I knew she would not approve of me making a choice of adoption without discussing it with Benjamin, and Vinny. This secret has been hanging over my head and weighing on me for years. Benjamin's phone call was very timely. I had been thinking about the relationship I was trying to build with Darien, and I knew that in order for it to work, I would have to be honest with him and tell him about the baby I gave up for adoption.

When Benjamin called to cancel earlier, he said he would be getting back in touch with me in a few weeks. I was hopeful that he would because I needed this to be out in the open before Darien got back from Florida. I was going to lay low while he was away but when he got back, I was going to let him know that I wanted more from our relationship. I know we both said we were not looking for anything serious, but it seemed like we both enjoyed ourselves the other night, and I'm hoping that I can change his mind. I thought about calling Darien after sitting around for hours thinking about everything. It was very late and I knew he would have to work in the morning. I decided I would call him tomorrow.

At first when Darien told me he was going to on the road a lot over the next thirty days or so, I was a little upset, but now with all this recent drama with Benjamin showing up out of the blue, I was glad Darien was away.

Journal Entry
Thursday

I didn't get a chance to call Benjamin back to confirm our meeting. I planned most of the day what I would say, and how I wanted our first meeting in over seven years to go. Just when I thought I had my emotions under control enough to call him to confirm and plan when and where we would meet, he called me to cancel. He merely said something came up. I cannot believe it. I mean he walked back into my life after all these years and asked to see me, then all of a sudden something has come up and he cannot meet with me. I guess I should be thankful that he called, and didn't just disappear, as he did before. All I know is that I have to see him and talk to him. His phone call out of the blue really affected me and I need to open up to him about everything. There are too many things left unsaid, and unknown, between us for either of us to be able to move on into healthy relationships. I really like Darien and want to be able to close the Benjamin chapter in my life, so that I can move onto whatever is next for me.

Darien

I sat in my hotel room thinking about Toni, after I finished reviewing my notes from my meetings today. I wondered why I had not been able to get in touch with her for the past day or so. I was a little disappointed because I really had considered going home for the weekend to see her, and I expected her to be blowing my phone up every day like most of the women I went out, with ended up doing. She was behaving a lot different than I was used to. Even when she called me the other night, she seemed very reserved and not pushy. Although I had decided to stay the weekend to get some work done, I really didn't want to work all weekend. I thought about trying to find a nice club or something to go to, tomorrow night.

Even though Toni continued to creep into my mind, I was not caught up, as Vince would say. She was just a nice girl, and we had both agreed in the beginning, we didn't want anything serious. Going to a club should not be an issue since we were casual anyway. I thought about asking this cute girl from the office to go with me. She has been flirting with me all week, offering to get my lunch for me every day. Maybe that's what I needed another woman to erase Toni out of my mind. She was in my subconscious because she was the last woman I took out on a date. I decided to ask Rosa out tomorrow and see what happened. If she said no, then I would go alone. I made a note to check in with Vince tomorrow, also, to let him know I was on the prowl again, in Miami. He seemed to think Toni had gotten to me and I was going soft or something. I had to let him know that was not the case.

Chapter 12

David

After talking to Benjamin, and, my father, I felt a sense of relief because I had a little more time before I would potentially have to face Jada, and tell the truth. I actually was hopeful that Toni would agree to keep quiet about Benjamin taking the blame for my crime. I was counting on her love and devotion for Jada to win over instead of doing what is right. My next issue was going to be how to explain to Jada how I got Benjamin to cancel his trip. She was going to want all the details, and obviously, I cannot tell her the truth. I could, however, tell her part of the truth, which was that I convinced him to take some time to think about what he was trying to accomplish, and to get himself established with a job, first.

Jada

David was home when I got in and I rushed to finish dinner. Thank goodness, I thought to throw some chicken in the Crockpot, this morning. After dinner, I quickly got the kids settled down for the night, so that David and I could talk. After the kids were in bed and I cleaned up the kitchen I came into the bedroom, and closed the door. David was reviewing paperwork, but he put it aside when I walked in.

"So," I said, "how did you convince Benjamin to back off and cancel his trip to see Toni?"

He looked up at me and said, "actually I had very little to do with it. When I called him, I simply asked him to think about what he was trying to accomplish, to consider holding off in order to think about the ramifications of his action, and to take some time to pull himself together. You know maybe get a job and a place to stay."

I sighed and said, "Thank God, because I was not ready to deal with all of this stuff this weekend. Hopefully once he thinks about everything, he will decide to stay away for good and leave us alone."

David reached out to grab me and pull me to him. He hugged me tightly for a moment. Then he released me and said, "Baby I agree that Benjamin's return is going to be very difficult, but I really think it's inevitable, so you need to prepare yourself for how you're going to handle things when Toni finds out that you knew where Benjamin was all this time."

I knew David was right, but I would have never kept anything from Toni if he had not asked me to. I thought about what David had said, and I also thought about the comments that Toni had made several times over the past few days, about their being things with she and Benjamin that I didn't know about. Maybe in the end, we both had secrets and she would not be able to hold this one over my head.

David Sr.

I was relieved that Benjamin had agreed to delay his meeting with Toni. Now all I had to do was come up with a job for him. I made a few phone calls after he left, and had a few possibilities that I needed to explore further over the next few days. I was trying to get him a job working with the Washington Wizards. Basketball was his passion, and although a job in the front office is not really, what he had dreamed of for himself, it would be a great paying job and he would be able to be close to the game he loved. I wanted to make sure that Benjamin was happy, so I could keep him right where I wanted him.

After he left my office, I also made a few phone calls to check on the young lady who was involved in the incident. I had kept close tabs on her over the years also. Since Benjamin had been released, she had been notified I wanted to make sure she kept up her end of the deal; not to contact anyone involved in the case. The last thing I needed was her coming around stirring up trouble. I also had to keep a close eye on the sports reporter who was determined to get the inside story on what happened to the rising star, Benjamin Royal. It had been easy to plant the story of a career ending injury to most of the sports reporters, but there was one young woman who put up quite a fight. In the end, I ended up having to pull some strings to have her transferred to California, and pay her a small amount of money to drop the story. For the moment, everything seemed to be under control.

Vince

I had a very productive day and felt very good about my music career. I was managing a few small bands and I had made progress on getting some gigs lined up for them in the coming months. I also had worked on my own music over the last few days and had come up with some catchy jingles for a few commercials. I was so excited about all of this and could not wait for Gina to come home. We had talked earlier that day and tonight we were going to be at my place, which was great, because I wanted her to hear my new songs. I decided to cook dinner. As Darien frequently reminded me, she really was a terrible cook and I was not in the mood for any take out tonight. I could not understand why she could not cook. Her mother was an excellent cook. We went to her house every Sunday, after church, for dinner and Gina was always in the kitchen with her while she cooked. She obviously was not paying any attention, because she could barely boil water.

I decided to make some fish, and steam some vegetables, one of Gina's favorites. When Gina arrived, she looked very upset. She had obviously been crying. All of my excitement over my productive day went out the window. I spent the better part of an hour listening to how her new boss had been treating her as if she didn't know anything and she wanted to quit and look for another job. I knew Gina's moods very well. This felt like a pre- menstrual mood. As she cried and talked about everything, I looked at the calendar and tried to remember where she was in her cycle. I tried and finally found a lull in her tirade to ask the question, "Gina, honey is this your period week?"

She stopped and glared at me and said, "No Vince, it's not and that's not the answer every time I get upset."

I started rubbing her hand that I had been holding this entire time and said, "Gina, I was just asking because you normally get very emotional around that time and I actually can't remember the last time you had your period."

She sniffled, pulled her hand away from mine, and got up from the couch where we had been sitting. She went to her briefcase and started flipping through her day planner. She kept flipping the pages back for what seemed like forever. The further back she went the whiter her face got. Finally, she stopped and turned to me and said, "Oh my God, Vince. It has been over two months since I had my period. I've been so busy trying to please my new boss; I didn't even realize that I missed my period last month."

I jumped off the couch and starting pacing and said, "Gina, are you trying to tell me that you might be pregnant?"

She was shaking her head and mouthing the word 'no' but no sound was coming out of her mouth. I, too, was speechless. *This is not happening to me*, I thought to myself. I mean I love Gina, but I was not ready to be a husband, or a father. We were both just standing there staring at each other for a long time. I decided to take the lead on this one.

"Gina, okay, let's not over react. Let us just get a test and see what it says. Don't women sometimes miss their period when they're under a lot of stress?"

She was still crying. I could see the tears streaming down her cheeks and she said, "Yes, Vince, You're right. I have been really stressed, so maybe that's it. I will get a test tomorrow and we will see."

I went over to her, embraced her, and whispered into her ear, "Gina, baby, no matter what the test says we will talk about what we both want to do, and it will be okay."

Gina just held me close and said, "I know Vince, everything will be okay."

Gina decided to go back to her place. At first, I protested, but then I was relieved because I needed some time to gather myself, and my emotions. I meant what I told her. If she was pregnant, we would sit down and talk about what we both felt was best. However, I was not ready for parenthood, or being someone's husband. I loved Gina, and I know that one day I will be married to her and we will have children, but I have to be ready. I'm doing okay right now with managing the bands and picking up some jobs making music for commercials, but I'm in no position to handle the responsibilities of a family. I hope Gina understood that. Gina said she would call me in the morning after she took the test. She was going to pick up one on her way home tonight.

Gina

My evening with Vince didn't go exactly as planned. I underestimated how in tuned Vince was to my moods, and my cycle. I was venting to him about my boss, and the drama at work, and he asked my about my period. I acted surprised, but came clean about the possibility of me being pregnant. I already knew I was, and was hoping to keep it from him a little longer. Now I was going to have to confirm the pregnancy tomorrow and start the entire charade of deciding what we should do. I already knew what we were going to do. We were getting married and having a child.

I've been planning this for the past few months. I love Vince and I know he loves me, but he has an unrealistic expectation of what he needs to be in order to marry me. He keeps saying he wants to be prepared. Well I was ready, and now with the baby coming, he was going to have to get ready. Even though I already had a home pregnancy test and confirmation from the free clinic, I was going to stop and get another one and take it again tomorrow. I needed to be prepared to show him the proof tomorrow.

Chapter 13

Darien

I was sound asleep when the plane touched down in Harrisburg. I quickly gathered my belongings and waited patiently for the announcement that we could exit the plane. I was so happy to be home for the weekend. The past week flew by. I was happy to be back to see my mom and lil sis, Joy, and have a date planned with Toni tomorrow night. Toni and I've been talking every night for the past week.. I was really enjoying her conversation and I looked forward to our dinner date. I had gone out to a club with a girl from the office down in Miami, but I really didn't enjoy myself at all. My plan was to do what I always did, spend a little time at the club, buy her a few drinks, and then take her back to my hotel room for a real freak fest. Well it didn't turn out that way. Actually after we left the club, I took her home. I didn't know what was wrong with me, but I just was not interested in the whole game right now. I was very pleased when Toni called me on Sunday morning, and we've talked everyday since. I actually look forward to talking to her each day. Maybe Vince was right, she had gotten under my skin. I was meeting Vince for drinks tonight, as soon as I left the airport; I was going to meet him downtown. He called me a few days ago and said we had to talk when I got home. In fact, he insisted that I come back this weekend because he had to speak to me in person. It could not wait. I had no idea what was going on with him, but it had to be something pretty serious because he sounded very different on the phone. As soon as I retrieved my bag and got into my car, I called Vince to confirm where we were meeting. Vince answered, "Hey man. Are you on your way yet?"

"Yes," I answered. "Just got into my car and I'm headed your way now. You still want me to meet you at the spot on Second Street.?"

"Yeah. I'm already here and I got us a booth towards the back. I'll be waiting for you when you get here." He sounded stressed out. I was getting really concerned about what might be going on with him.

"Okay man."

"I will be there in about fifteen to twenty minutes."

Toni

The week flew by. I was back at work and had put all thoughts of Benjamin out of my mind for now. I already knew what I had to do once he contacted me again. I decided that I would give him thirty days. If he didn't get back in touch with me by then, I was going to call him and tell him that we had to talk. Things seemed to be moving in the right direction with Darien. We talked every day this week, and he was coming home this weekend to see me. Jada seemed very happy about all of this. Any mention of Benjamin and she became a different person. She was very pleased with the fact that I was continuing to pursue something more with Darien. I had been feeling a little tired and sluggish all week. I had some kind of stomach bug or something for a few days last week and over the weekend. Seems like it went away, but the fatigue was still there. I left work a little early, so that I could get my nails and hair done before Darien got back in town. Just as I was pulling into the salon, my cell phone rang. I didn't even look at the phone before I answered. "Hello."

"Hey there pretty lady," Darien said.

I was grinning from ear to ear. His call surprised me, as I didn't expect to hear from him until tomorrow. He said he would call me to let me know what time he was picking me up for our date on Saturday.

"Hey Darien, this is a surprise to hear from you today. I thought you were getting in later."

"No, I was actually able to get an earlier flight. I just got in and am on my way to meet my boy Vince for a drink, before I head over to visit my mom and 'lil' sis."

"Oh, that's cool. I'm glad you made it back safely and I'm looking forward to seeing you tomorrow."

He cleared his throat and said, "Well actually I was calling to see if maybe I could stop over to see you tonight, if it's not too late when I leave my mom's house."

I thought for about 2 seconds before I said, "Oh sure that would be great. Just give me a call okay?" I could hear him smiling through the phone and then he said, "Good, cause I really didn't want to have to wait until tomorrow to see you. I'll give you a call a little later. Okay?"

Now it was my turn to smile again. "Yes, Darien just give me a call later when You're on your way."

*   *   *   *   *   *   *   *

I was cheesing like a Cheshire cat when I walked into the salon. I walked up to the counter and said, "I have an appointment for hair and nails, but I need to add some waxing services also." The girl behind the counter checked the book and tried to see where she could fit me in. All the while, I was thinking about what a wonderful weekend Darien and I were going to have. It has been two weeks and my body had really missed him.

Darien

I walked in and saw Vince sitting in the back just like he said. He was drinking already and when I approached him, he sat with his head in hands. I stood back for a minute, before I approached him, because he almost looked like he might be praying and I didn't want to interrupt him.

"Hey Vince," I finally said.

He looked up, his eyes were completely bloodshot, and he looked like he had been drinking for days. "Hey man," he said back to me.

"Whoa! Vince, man, you look like crap. What's going on?"

He just started shaking his head, and took another sip of his beer, then he said, "Man if you only knew the week I've had, this week."

I sat down and poured myself a glass of beer out of the half-empty pitcher then said, "Man what's going on? Did something happen with you and Gina?" That was the only thing I could think of that would bring my boy down like this.

YESTERDAY'S LIES   Terri D.

He sat back in his chair and said, "I don't even know where to begin man."

I put my drink down and said, "Start at the beginning. I have as much time as you need."

He finally said almost in a whisper, "Man, Gina is pregnant."

I was not sure why this was such bad news for Vince. I mean as far as I was concerned he and Gina were already married so I thought this would be a good thing. Finally, I responded, "Oh, and obviously you're not happy about this?"

He slammed his fist down on the table and said, "Hell no, I'm not happy man. I'm not ready to be a husband or a father. This is not how I had everything planned out."

I had to think for a minute on how to respond. Clearly, he was very upset, and I was surprised by his response. I felt like we had reversed roles, or something, for a minute. I was thinking he would be talking me down off the roof of the tallest building, if I were in his shoes right now. I never thought he would be so distraught over this. "Okay, so what are you and Gina going to do?" I asked.

He was shaking his head again and had put his head down on the table. Then he looked up and said, "That's the problem man. We are both on opposite sides of this issue. I'm not ready and Gina is ecstatic and has damned near planned the wedding already."

"Wow," I said as I poured myself another glass of beer and motioned for the server to refill our pitcher. "So, she wants to get married and you want what, exactly?"

"Man, I don't know. Gina flipped out on me when I didn't immediately drop down on one knee, and ask for her hand."

111

I was trying to figure out a tactful way to ask him why he was so opposed to it, especially since they were living the *almost-married life* anyway. "Vince let me ask you a question. Try not to get upset, okay?"

"Well that depends on what the question is," he answered.

I sighed heavily and then said, "Well I'm just curious why you're so upset, and so opposed to marriage, when you and Gina are basically married anyway. I mean don't you sleep together every night?" He nodded, yes, and I continued, "And don't you spend all of your free time together?" Again, he nodded, yes. "So, I don't get it. What is it about actually marrying her that bothers you so much?"

He thought for a minute and then finally answered, "Darien, I take my responsibility as a husband and father very seriously. I love Gina with all my heart and I do plan to marry her one day. It's just that I do not feel that I'm ready to have that responsibility. My music career is going okay, but I'm not in a financial position to care for a wife, and a child, right now."

I was nodding now. "Okay I get it. So, you're concerned about being able to care for her financially?"

"Yes."

"Vince, maybe you need to put your plans on hold for a minute and get a steady job."

Vince looked at me as if I had just punched him in his gut. "Darien, my music is my life. I can't imagine what else I would do if I were not making music."

I was thinking to myself that he is being very selfish and narrow-minded right now. Again, I felt that we had changed roles, or something, because he was really acting like the selfish person he always accused me of being. There was no beating around the bush on this one. I had to let my boy know that he was being completely unreasonable, especially since he loved Gina. This would be a very different conversation if this were some girl he just met, but he has been with Gina over three years now. I took a big swig of my beer before I started.

"Vince, I have to be totally honest with you man. I think you're being totally selfish right now." He started to interrupt me, but I put my hand up to stop him, "hold on let me finish. You say you love Gina and you guys have been together over three years. You said you plan to marry her anyway, so guess what? Your plans just got rearranged a bit because you have a baby on the way by the woman you love. You need to suck it up and do whatever you need to do to make a way to provide for your new family. That's it plain and simple."

After I finished Vince just sat there drinking his beer looking across the table at me for a few minutes. Then finally, he said, "You know what man? You're right. I do not know what the hell is wrong with me. I love Gina and we are going to have a baby." I was nodding my head while I took a swig of my beer. "So Darien, will you be my best man?" Vince asked.

I answered, "Well that depends."

He looked surprised, and said, "On what?"

"Gina, and if she still wants to get married. You said she was pretty upset with you. How do you plan to smooth things over with her?" I asked.

Vince thought for a moment and said, "I'm not sure, but I'm going to go straight to her place, when I leave here, to talk this over with her. I cannot believe I was being such an ass."

I thought the same thing, but didn't want to rub it in. We finished our pitcher of beer and I briefly filled him in on things with Toni and me. He was looking much better now, and wanted to go see Gina right away. We both walked out together, and he promised to call me tomorrow to let me know how things went with Gina tonight.

I called my mom, as soon as I got to my car, to let her know I was on my way. I also told her that my visit tonight was going to be brief, but I wanted to check in on her and Joy. She sounded happy to hear from me and excited I was coming by but assured me that both she and Joy were doing fine. Mom didn't live far from where Vince and I had met so I was still on the phone with her when I pulled up in front of her house. I saw my little sister sitting on the front porch with a few of her friends. She ran to the car when she saw me. When I got out, she gave me a great big hug and told me how much she missed me. She also started on about how much she loved her school. Mom, and I, had been discussing sending her to a private boarding school. I was not happy with the public schools, and the crowd that Joy was gravitating towards, now that she was going to high school.

"Joy," I said," We will talk about the school situation later in private, you, mom, and me. Not out in public in front of your friends."

She pouted and said, "Okay big brother, but please let me at least try going to public high school and if it doesn't work out I can go to private school."

I hugged her to me and said, "We'll see, but no promises." This made her happy and she ran back over to her friends and started laughing and giggling with them again. Before I even walked into the house, I could tell my mom had spent the entire day in the kitchen. I was shaking

114

my head and I walked towards her to give her a hug and said, "Mom, I told you not to cook for me."

She gave me a big squeeze and said, "I have to eat too, so don't think this is all for you."

I smiled and said, "Okay mom, but I know you made all of my favorites didn't you?'

She didn't respond, but I could tell by the smell and the look on her face, I was right.

I sat down at the table and she fixed me a healthy plate. Everything was delicious. The last great home cooked meal I had, was the breakfast Toni had fixed for me, almost two weeks ago. My mother was very pleased at how much I ate. While I ate, she brought me up to date on all of the latest neighborhood gossip, and she let me know that Joy was behaving herself, at least for now. That was good news, but I was sure it was Joy's attempt at keeping us from demanding she change schools. My mom and I talked for an hour, or so, before I decided to make my exit. I promised to come by on Sunday, before I left for the airport to say good-bye. Mom wanted me to take several plates of food with me, but I refused. I told her I had plans with a friend for dinner tomorrow, and I would never get to eat it all before I left. She looked disappointed, but she understood.

After I left mom's house, I went back to check on my place, and shower and change. I called Toni on my way to my house, to let her know I would be over in about an hour. She sounded excited to see me, and I could not wait to see her too. Maybe Vince was right, and I was going soft or something, because I could not get Toni out of my mind; thoughts of her and the last time we were together, consumed my thoughts. It seems like everything, and everyone, reminded me of Toni lately.

115

YESTERDAY'S LIES

Terri D.

Chapter 14

Toni

Darien called me to let me know he would be over within an hour. I had candles all around my room and in the bathroom. Also, I had created a new playlist on my *iPod* for us to listen to. Darien said he had already eaten, so I didn't have to worry about feeding him any dinner. I had been thinking for the past few hours about how I wanted my time with Darien to go this weekend. I thought about telling him about the baby I gave up, but then thought that maybe it was way too soon for us to talk about things like that. I really wanted to get a sense of where he thought our relationship was headed. I decided to play the entire evening by ear, based upon his actions.

Darien

I thought about the situation with my boy Vince and Gina all the way over to Toni's house. I really hoped that things were going to work out for them, and I hoped that Vince was going to make the right decision because, he wanted to and not because of the things I had said to him. I chuckled to myself as I thought about Vince getting married and being a father. I always knew he would be the first to get married. Asking me to be his best man flattered me. Of course, I would stand beside my boy, as he took his vows and made one of the biggest decisions of his life. The only concern I had was Gina. She and I really didn't get along that well and I'm sure she would protest me being Vince's best man, but that was between the two of them. Truth be told I really didn't get a good vibe from her either. Something about her always rubbed me the wrong way, but Vince loved her and he had to deal with her on a daily basis, not me. If he needed me, I would be there. As I pulled up in front of Toni's house, a smile came over my face as I imagined what she had planned for me tonight. I really liked how she had set the mood the last time with the candles, and the music was on point. I walked up to the door and rang the doorbell. Toni answered the door, looked stunning as usual, and was smiling from ear to ear. I stepped inside and said, "Girl what are you cheesing so hard for?"

She laughed and said, "Boy why you playing? Give me a hug."

I pulled her to me and hugged her, then pulled back to plant a kiss on her waiting lips. She grabbed my hand and walked towards her living room. We sat down on the couch and she continued to hold my hand in hers.

"So," I said, "Seems like you missed me a little bit huh?"

She rolled her eyes while still smiling and said, "Now don't go getting a big head or anything, but yes two weeks is a long time to go without seeing you and I did miss you." She leaned towards me and touched my face and said, "You look very tired and worn out."

I turned my head slightly, kissed her hand, and said, "Yes, it was a long day and traveling always wears me out. Also, I mentioned to you that I was meeting my friend Vince for drinks when I got here and he's going through some stuff right now."

Toni looked very concerned and said, "Oh, well I hope it's nothing too serious. Is he going to be okay?"

I thought for a minute and said, "Yes I think so. I gave him some advice that I'm probably the last person in the world he should listen to. I'm not sure how it's going to go." I thought about telling Toni what was going on to get the female perspective on the situation, but decided against it because it really was not my business to tell. I decided to change the subject and said, "Yes I'm sure everything will be fine. So how have things been for you?"

Toni moved her hand from mine and shifted on the couch a little bit before she answered, "I've been fine, was a little under the weather for a few days, but I'm feeling better now."

"Oh?" I probed. "Is that why I was unable to reach you for a few days? You were out sick."

She shook her head yes, and then said, "Yes I was out for a few days with a stomach bug, or something, and I also had some other personal stuff I was dealing with as well."

I thought about her 'personal stuff' comment and immediately thought about how much I hated drama. I said, "Oh well I hope you were able to get everything taken care of now, and you look better physically."

Toni hesitated for a minute and then said, "Um, well, yes, I'm better physically, still just a little more tired than usual, but not sick to my stomach like I had been. As for the personal stuff it's not resolved yet, but it will be very soon."

"Well that's good. I hope you're able to get everything resolved quickly."

Toni

Darien looked great and I had not realized really how much I had missed him until I opened the door and saw him. I was a little embarrassed that I was smiling so much when I saw him; he noticed it, and teased me about. Now it seemed like he was a little preoccupied and tired. Maybe he is disappointed that I didn't meet him at the door naked, and ready to jump his bones. I think I need to move things along in the direction I want them to go in for the evening. I'm going to move us upstairs to the bedroom and actually suggest that I draw us a nice hot bath.

Darien

I was thinking about how things might be going with Vince and Gina. Toni must have noticed my daydreaming and said, "Darien if you're tired and want to take a rain check on tonight that's fine."

I moved closer to her on the couch, grabbed her hands again, and said, "No, Toni's it's not that. I'm sorry, but my friend is over his girlfriend's house right now talking to her, and I was just thinking that I wondered how it was going."

"Oh," she said. "Well how about this? I will draw us a nice hot bath- you and I can soak in the tub to relax awhile.

You're tired and we can get a good night's sleep and catch up on lost time enjoying each other tomorrow."

A hot bath and good night's sleep sounded like music to my ears. I stood up and said,
"Lead the way my dear."

While Toni ran the bath in the bathroom, I undressed and checked my cell phone one last time, before I turned it off to see if Vince had text messaged me about his meeting with Gina. I didn't have any messages, so I turned my phone off and prepared myself to enjoy what Toni had in store for me.

Toni

I finished preparing the bath for Darien and I, and decided to slip into the tub alone and then call him into the bathroom. I moved my *iPod* into the bathroom, called for Darien to join me, and then started the music using my remote. When Darien stepped into the bathroom completely naked, the sight of his naked body, in the candle light, took my breath away. This man was damned near perfect in every way. I motioned for Darien to join me in the tub in front of me. I wanted him to lie back, so that I could give him a nice shoulder massage while we soaked and relaxed in the tub. Darien made his way over to the tub and got into position. I started to massage his shoulders and he immediately started to moan with pleasure. I whispered in his ear, "How does that feel baby?"

He moaned again and said, "This is wonderful Toni. I didn't realize how tired and stressed I was. This is perfect."

Smiling I said, "Good, I'm glad you're enjoying yourself, Darien. I really did miss not seeing you the past two weeks. So, how are things going down there? When do you think you will be back?"

He shifted a little, so that he could turn his head and then responded, "Things are going pretty well. I think we should be able to complete the audit within the next two to three weeks."

I was happy to hear that he might be back home in a few weeks, but was a little disappointed that he didn't say he missed me too.

Darien

I really had missed Toni, too. I was not going to tell her that though, because I still needed to try to get my brain around why she was affecting me this way. It's not like she is the first nice girl I've met, or anything. I was enjoying myself, but I almost felt like I was not in control of my body, or emotions, and I didn't like feeling that way at all. She was taking over all of my thoughts. I thought about Toni when I was not working or alone, and not just in a sexual way. When I was eating, I thought about the wonderful breakfast she had made for me. When I was listening to the radio, there were songs that she had played that night that made me think of her. I had never thought about a woman like this before. My only thoughts were when I could get *it*, initially, and if *it* was good when I would get *it* again. Sitting in a tub soaking like this with candles and soft music, this was definitely on the *oh, hell no!* list prior to Toni. Vince had me half way convinced that she was running a game, or something on me, but everything felt sincere and straight from her heart. It's funny he would say that about Toni, and he has never met her, because I'm not so sure about his girl Gina. The more I thought about this pregnancy situation the more I thought it might be a set up because she was tired of waiting for him.

Gina had been very disappointed this past Valentines' day when Vince didn't pop the question. Even though my instincts were telling me this situation was a little too convenient, I still stood by what I said to him earlier. If he loves her and plans to marry her one day, anyway, he should go ahead and handle his business now.

Toni

I wanted to ask Darien what was next for us, but I decided to just let that conversation alone for now, and once he was back home for good I would discuss that with him. Besides, by then this whole mess with Benjamin should be over, and I can talk to him about that too. We continued to lie in the tub and I rubbed his shoulders and arms. We didn't talk much just listened to music and enjoyed being close to each other. I re-filled the tub several times because the water started to get cold. Finally, when I heard Darien start to snore a bit, I knew he was toast, and it was time for us to go to bed. I gently nudged him and he woke up and said, "Oh Toni I'm so sorry, how rude of me to fall asleep on you like that."

I laughed and said, "It's okay, Darien, I know You're tired. Let's get out of here and head to bed so we can both get some sleep."

He yawned and said, "Okay and I promise I will make it up to you in the morning before I leave."

Now that was one promise I was hoping he would keep, because I was really in the mood for some good loving tonight, but was willing to wait until the morning, when he was fully rested.

Darien was true to his word, and woke me up with something extra special after a good nights sleep. I had planned to make him a big breakfast again, but since we didn't get out of the bed until almost 1 in the afternoon, I had to change my plans a little bit. Darien wanted to go to his house and check on his friend, and said he would call me about dinner. I offered to make us dinner, but he said he wanted to make sure everything was cool with his friend first. He didn't want me to start making dinner and then there be a change in plans. I understood and told him to just give me a call, and let me know if we were going to get a chance to see each other again before he left. The way he held me and kissed me before he left; it made me feel like he had missed me, even though he didn't say it. I also got the feeling that he wanted to make sure he saw me again before he left. All of this made me smile, even more. I wanted Darien and planned to do whatever I needed to do to make sure that this time, if I found love, it would not get away from me.

Darien

As soon as I got to my car, I turned on my phone to check for messages. I only had one and it was from Vince. It was very brief. He just asked me to call him when I got a chance. I tried to determine by the sound of his voice how things had gone with Gina, but I was not able to, just from his message. I dialed his number as I started to drive. He answered right away and sounded out of breath.

"Hey Man," I said. "So how did it go?"

"Look I'm at the gym, so let me call you back when I'm finished with my workout, okay?"

Well that was a good sign. That he was at the gym. I said, "You know what man? I think I'm going to come over there. I need to work out a little myself. So I'll see you in about fifteen minutes."

"Okay man, I'll see you when you get here."

I drove straight to the gym from Toni's house. I already had some clothes in my trunk I could change into to work out in. When I got to the gym and changed, I went over to the weights, where I knew Vince would be. He was just about finished with his routine, when I walked up. He looked much better than he had last night when I saw him. There were not a lot of people in the gym today, so I felt comfortable asking him how things went with Gina. I said, "So man, how did it go?"

He started shaking his head and smiling, "Man this woman is a trip."

I said, "What do you mean? Is she making you beg, or buy her a big ring, or something?"

"No, it's just that when I got to her house last night, I thought I walked into one of those bridal magazines or something. Even though the last time we saw each other, I told her absolutely no to getting married, she had started planning the entire thing."

Now I was shaking my head and wondering again if this entire thing might have been a set up or not. He continued, "She was very happy to see me and accepted my apology right away. She said she knew I would come to my senses, and she immediately started telling me about all the plans she had made. She wants to pull everything together in the next sixty days. She is adamant that we get married before she starts to show. She does not want to look fat in her wedding dress."

I sat down and said, "Wow, man. Are you sure you're going to be ready for all of this in the next two months?"

"I don't know man, but you're the one who told me to suck it up and do what's right. So I've got to do right by Gina now."

I was afraid he was going to make this my decision so I said, "Look Vince you have to make this decision because you want to. Not because I said it's what you should do."

His expression changed and he looked concerned and said, "So you don't think I should marry her?"

I let out a heavy sigh and said, "Vince it's not my decision to make. You have to decide what you're comfortable with. All I'm saying is that you say you love Gina, and you're always with her, so you're practically married anyway. To me it seems like the logical thing to do."

He thought for a minute then said, "Well I do love Gina and I do want to marry her. The only reason I freaked out initially, is because I don't feel financially ready for this responsibility."

I interrupted and said, "For that man you know I can help you review your finances, and come up with a budget.

Also you need to think about which place to keep and which one to sell."

Vince was starting to look like he was going to faint or something. I suggested that we leave and go grab a bite to eat, so we could continue our conversation. I also wanted to get more information from him on exactly what Gina had already planned. The more I heard, the more concerned I became about this being a set up. Vince was a great guy, and didn't deserve to get caught up like this even though he said he loved her, she should not be playing games with him like this. Maybe Vince was right about Toni too. Maybe she had me caught up in some female mind game.

YESTERDAY'S LIES   Terri D.

Chapter 15

Gina

Things were moving along as expected with Vince. After we officially confirmed the pregnancy, we went through several days of discussion on what to do. I made it very clear on day one that an abortion was not an option I was willing to entertain. I pushed the marriage issue a little too hard initially and he was not feeling it. We had a huge fight and didn't talk for two days. Finally, last night he showed up, and said he agreed that we should get married. I knew he would come around eventually, but never thought it would be a talk with his dog of a friend, Darien, that would bring him to this conclusion. I almost laughed out loud in his face when he told me that Darien had convinced him to do the right thing. Mr. Booty calls himself going to tell someone they should get married.

Anyway, I didn't care how it happened, I just know that I want to marry Vince have his baby and that's what is going to happen. I was moving forward full speed ahead with my plans. I had my dress already and was going to be securing the church and reception location next week. I already spoke to my mother and she was working on getting the budget approved from my father. My mother was a little less than thrilled especially about the baby part and she liked Vince, but said he was not really husband material. She didn't like the fact that he didn't have a 'real' job. Vince being a musician/producer was a foreign concept to my mother. She wanted him to be a doctor like my father or a lawyer.

I loved Vince and hated having to trick him into marrying me this way, but he just needed a little nudge in this direction. I know he loves me, but his crazy ideas about what it takes to be a husband and father, were driving me insane. We are going to spend the next week finalizing the plans for the wedding, and we are going to my first official prenatal appointment. According to my calculations, I should be about twelve weeks along by now. I was not sure which I was more excited about the wedding planning or the baby. It didn't matter as long as I ended up married to Vince and having his baby I would be the happiest woman in the world.

Vince

Darien insisted we grab a bite and talk more about my situation with Gina. We drove our separate cars to the restaurant. As I was driving, I was really feeling good about everything today. I knew what I needed to do and was willing to do it. I know this was not exactly according to my plan, but I loved Gina and I knew that we belonged together. We had a rough patch a few months ago right after Valentine's Day. She was very disappointed and upset that I didn't propose to her then. She had gotten it into her head that I was going to and when I didn't, it shattered her world. We were apart for about four to six weeks but I never told anyone. She stayed at her place; I stayed at mine and worked on my music. We talked frequently and emailed from time to time, but she just told me that she was very disappointed that we had been dating so long, and I still was not ready to marry her. It's funny I cannot even remember how we ended up getting back together really. It's like one day she showed up and said okay you win Vince. We do not have to get married right now. We can wait until you're ready and that was it. Just as I was thinking about all of this, it occurred to me that this pregnancy could have been a set up. As quickly as the thought came into my mind, I dismissed it. Gina would never play a game like that with me. She was too nice of a girl, and she did seem totally taken by surprise when we first thought she might be pregnant.

Darien

I followed Vince to our favorite wing spot. We were going to get some wings and a beer to finish our conversation. I wanted to get a little more information from him on exactly what Miss Gina had already planned. I was getting the feeling *little miss goody two shoes* was trying to play my man. On the way to the wing spot, I called Toni and let her know that we were on for dinner. I told her it was her choice, and to pick something nice. I could hear her smile through the phone. Funny thing was as soon as I heard her voice I smiled too.

We got to the spot, got a table, and continued our conversation. I think Vince had picked up on my concern because now he seemed a little more reserved and closed mouthed about the details. I did find out that they planned to finish making the arrangements next week. They were both taking the week off, and they were going to be going to their first prenatal appointment. He did seem excited or maybe it was nervous about the baby part of this equation. By the time we had finished our plates of wings, and a pitcher of beer, I felt a lot better. It seemed like Vince had a good plan, and was making the decision because he wanted to, not because of pressure from Gina or me. I did ask him if Gina had objected to me being the best man. He laughed and said, "Hell no man. She has no say so on that at all."

So, it seemed like there was going to be a wedding in the next two months. He was going to confirm the actual date for me next week, once they got everything set. I already knew who my date was going to be. Vince said I absolutely had to bring a date because Gina didn't want me single, and on the prowl, during the reception. I knew that comment came directly from her, but it didn't bother me at all. I knew I wanted to take Toni to the wedding; I just needed the date, so I could have her pencil me in on her calendar.

Toni

I was feeling very good about how things went with Darien last night. I was going to hang back and be supportive and caring, but not too pushy, about being in an official relationship right now. My mother used to tell me to focus on a man's actions not the words coming out of his mouth. In this situation, I felt very comfortable with Darien's actions even though he didn't seem to be willing to admit that he is interested in me or wants something more.

I kept myself busy around the house most of the afternoon and patiently waited for Darien to call to let me know about tonight. I thought about calling Jada, but since the Benjamin phone call, things with her have been a little strained. Seems like she really does not want me to talk to Benjamin, and it's weird, because all of these years she has been the one telling me I need to have closure on that relationship. How else to get closure than to actually talk to or see the person and get everything off your chest? Just when I was thinking about getting something to eat, my phone rang and it was Darien. He said we were on for dinner and I was to pick the restaurant. He said do something later like 7:30 or 8:00 because he was just having a quick bite for lunch now and it was almost 3:00.

I decided to call Jada, while I fixed myself a little fruit salad to hold me over until tonight. Jada would know the perfect place for us to go to have a nice dinner. I dialed her number and she answered on the third ring

"Hey girlie," she said. "What's been going on with you? I barely saw you in the office last week at all."

"I know. I was really busy trying to get caught up from the days I missed the previous week. How are David and the kids doing?" I could hear the kids in the background making a bunch of noise. It sounded like they were playing a game or something.

"They're all doing fine. They're playing the Wii right now, driving me crazy with all that noise. So what have you been up to?"

"Well Darien came home this weekend, which is why I'm calling. I wanted your suggestion for a nice restaurant for us to go to for dinner tonight."

"Oh, well things are going well for you guys then huh?"

I was smiling and said, "Yes I think so. I mean we still have not talked about what's next or anything like that, but we talk or email each other every day and he came home this weekend to see me."

"Well that's great Toni. I'm glad you have been able to keep your mind off of Benjamin."

I was instantly irritated and sorry I called her. I do not know why she was suddenly against Benjamin. Anyway, I decided not to react to her comment and just wanted to get what I needed from her and get off the phone. "So, do you have any good suggestions for a nice restaurant?"

She thought for a minute and said, "Yes actually I do. There is this nice little place called Sasha's it's off of Linglestown Road. I met one of my clients there for lunch last week. Never heard of it or been there before, but it was really good and the atmosphere would be perfect for you and Darien."

I wrote down the name, confirmed the location, and ended the call with Jada. I told her we would catch up one day next week at the office. After I got off the phone with Jada, I looked up the number for the restaurant, called, and made reservations for 8:00 o'clock. I sent Darien a text letting him know we had reservations at 8:00, o'clock and he responded that he would pick me up at 7:30.

After eating my salad, I felt a little queasy again, so I decided to lie down and take a little nap before my dinner date with Darien. I was getting a little worried about this stomach thing lingering as long as it had, and if things didn't improve by next week, I was going to the doctor. I could barely eat anything except crackers and drink ginger ale without it making me feel sick to my stomach. When I got to my room, I sat on the edge of the bed looking around my room and remembering some of the intimate details of this morning with Darien. I could not stop smiling. I lay down and enjoyed my pleasant memories, as I drifted into a very deep sleep.

I could not believe the time on the clock when I woke up and saw it was 6:45 PM. Oh, my goodness, I thought to myself and jumped up. I had to get ready for my date with Darien. I had slept all afternoon. I felt refreshed, but a little dizzy from jumping up so quickly. I quickly showered and picked out a nice dress to wear. I didn't have time to curl my hair, so I just pulled it up into a nice tight bun, and chose some long dangling earrings to accent my neck since my hair was pulled up.

Darien

After I left Vince, I went home and just cleaned up a bit. I read over some of my notes from my meetings last week. I was very distracted. I was thinking about Toni. I was really looking forward to seeing her tonight, and dreaded leaving to go back to Florida this week. This woman was really getting under my skin. She was consuming all of my thoughts. This was crazy. I would love to be able to talk to Vince about all of this, but he has his own mess to deal with right now. After I gave up on working, I just put some music on and decided to relax a bit before I got ready to pick up Toni.

On my way over to Toni's house, I stopped at a red light and saw a flower stand. I remembered one time we were leaving her house, after lunch, and she mentioned that she loved her neighbor's flowers. I decided to pull over to see if I could find any like the ones she liked. I knew nothing about flowers, so I just walked around looking at all of them until I found some that looked like the ones Toni had pointed out that day. I purchased them and the lady told me they were called tulips. I smiled to myself, as I placed the flowers on the passenger seat of my car. I knew Toni would love them and it made me happy knowing she would enjoy them.

Toni

Darien arrived on time as usual, looked, and smelled even better than he did last night, if that's even possible. When I stepped forward to hug him, he pulled out the most beautiful flowers from behind his back I've ever seen. They were the most gorgeous tulips I had ever seen. I love tulips and could not ever remember telling him that.

Just when I was thinking that, he said, "I remember one time after lunch, when we were walking to our cars, you saw your neighbor's tulips, and you commented on how much you loved them. Don't ask me why, I remembered that, but I did just as I was driving past the flower stand down the street."

I was almost in tears. I said, "Darien they're beautiful and I don't care how or why you remembered I'm just glad you did."

I leapt at him and gave him a very long passionate kiss. He pushed me away after a few minutes and said, "Umm… if we are going to dinner we better leave now, before we end up ordering in."

I smiled and said, "Okay we can go to dinner now, but I have to put my flowers in some water first. Hold on a minute I will be right back."

I was on cloud nine as I walked to the kitchen to put my flowers in a nice vase. I knew things were certainly headed in the right direction with Darien. He would not, or could not, tell me how he felt, but I could feel it. His actions were speaking very loud and clear.

Darien

I knew she would love the flowers, but what I didn't expect was how good I would feel giving them to her and seeing her reaction. I had given flowers before, but it always felt like an obligation because the woman expected them on her birthday or Valentine's Day. It felt good to buy them for Toni just because I saw them, and thought of her. I heard her singing to herself in the kitchen as she put them in water. I also made a note to mention to her about my boy Vince, and the fact that he's musician. Her voice was beautiful and I felt certain he could help her, if she was interested in pursuing a singing career. I knew I had made her happy and I knew that tonight was going to be another special night for us. I was not ready to admit it to her, but she was growing on me, and I wanted to spend more time with her and get to know her better. Even though I said nothing serious when this all started, I was starting to think that maybe it was time for me to think about having something more with a woman besides sex on demand. It was funny because I really enjoyed Toni sexually, but I also enjoyed just spending time with her and talking to her. That's something I really have not allowed myself to do with anyone else.

Chapter 16

Toni

Journal Entry
Sunday

    I had the most amazing weekend ever with you. We ended up spending both Friday and Saturday night together. I thoroughly enjoyed myself. I enjoyed lying in your arms and falling asleep. Waking up still lying in your arms was even better than falling sleep that way. It was a wonderful feeling you next to me all night. I didn't sleep well, because I kept waking up to make sure I was not dreaming. Today was hard knowing that you had to leave and not being sure, when I would see you again. It was also hard not to bring up exactly what we are doing here. I mean this feels like a relationship, but the last time I tried to bring it up, you reminded me that we both agreed, when we starting hooking up, that we didn't want anything serious. I do not know why I just cannot let it go and let things just happen naturally. It's my impatience, I guess. I've got to work on that. For now, I'm very happy with how things are going for us. I will look forward to hearing from you while you're away. I've not heard from Benjamin again and I'm a little anxious. I really want to get that conversation with him over with, so I can move onto building something with Darien.

Darien

I had a great weekend. Spent most of it with Toni and I really enjoyed myself. She is a great girl. She is sexy, funny, and smart. She is the total package that men always say we are looking for in a woman. Who knew that you could actually find it? I was shaking my head to myself, when I thought about all the myths about woman that are floating around. I was most impressed with the fact that she didn't once bring up anything about our relationship. I was prepared for it, especially since we spent so much time together, but she didn't mention a word about it. The next surprise was that she didn't ask me when I was coming back or when she would see me again. She simply told me she enjoyed herself, and was looking forward to seeing me again. She is definitely different from what I was used to. The only thing I was not happy about was the fact that I didn't get a chance to see my boy Vince again this weekend. Even though he seemed okay on Saturday when I saw him, I wanted to check on him again before I left just to make sure nothing had changed.

Every time I thought about this situation, I smelled a rat. It was just all too convenient that Gina turned up pregnant, now, after the Valentines Day meltdown. I decided I would give him a few days, and if I didn't hear from him, I would call him to check in. I also wanted to get the date for the wedding from him, as soon as they set it, so I could make my arrangements to be home and to invite Toni to go with me.

Toni

I woke up with a smile on my face Monday morning. I was still on cloud nine because of the wonderful weekend I had with Darien. I know that Jada would be looking for a full report when I got to the office this morning. I got up and started to get ready, and all of a sudden, I was hit with a wave of nausea, out of nowhere. I had not eaten anything yet, and had a very light dinner last night. I rushed into the bathroom and stood there waiting for the feeling to pass. After a few minutes, it did, but as I stood there, waiting it occurred to me that I had not gotten my period yet, and I had been feeling very sick lately. My period was somewhat irregular, so it never bothered me when it was a little late. Darien and I had been very careful using condoms, except for one time when we ran out. I was not going to panic because it was probably nothing, but I did need to consider the possibility.

I finished getting ready for work. I sipped on ginger ale in order to keep my nausea under control. I decided to stop at the store on my way into the office to get a home pregnancy test. Even as I was thinking about it, I was dismissing it as a possibility. There was no way, I had been way too careful for this. It had to be my nerves because of work, and because of Benjamin calling me out of the blue. When I arrived at the office, I saw Jada's car so I knew she was already here. I contemplated telling her about the test I had purchased, but decided I would take the test and if it were positive, and then I would need Jada because I would not know how to handle that. Things with Darien were going well, but this could swing things in the absolute wrong direction. The last thing I needed would be for him to feel like I was trying to trap him.

141

I decided to go straight to the ladies' room on the first floor to take the test and get it out of the way. I didn't want to risk running into Jada, or anyone else for that matter. Right now I wanted the answer, so that I would know what my next move was going to be. I reached the rest room and was thankful that I was alone. I quickly made my way into the stall and read the instructions carefully before I took the test. I followed the instructions and waited with my eyes shut, praying a silent prayer for three minutes. Those three minutes felt like an eternity and when they were over, I opened one eye at a time. I stared at the test stick and could not believe my eyes. Before I knew it, I was standing up, throwing up in the toilet.. I was not sure, if I was sick to my stomach because the test was positive, or because I was pregnant.

Darien

I woke up thinking about Toni, and decided to send her a text message, before I got to the office and got too busy. The message simply said, *hey darling I was thinking about you and wanted you to know. I hope you have a wonderful day.* Clearly, I was getting in over my head with this woman and I needed to talk to my boy sooner, rather than later, about it. I had to admit I was out of my comfort zone now and needed some advice.

Toni

I heard my cell phone vibrating letting me know I had a text message. In between waves of nausea, I grabbed my phone and read the message from Darien. Immediately tears started flowing. I sat back down on the toilet, and sent a 911 message to Jada, telling her where to find me and to come as quickly as possible.

Jada

I had just started working on an important document when my cell phone rang. I picked it up and saw an urgent 911 message from Toni. I jumped up and headed for the ladies' room on the first floor. When I arrived, I found Toni standing by the sink washing her face. She motioned for me to lock the door behind me, and I did.

All kinds of thoughts were running through my head as to what today's crisis was about. I loved my girl Toni, but with her, there was always some drama of the day to deal with. Just then, she turned to me and extended her hand towards me, and I saw what she was holding in her hand. I gasped and brought both of my hands to my mouth to cover the shriek that I knew was coming.

David Sr.

I was making good progress with the job search for Benjamin. I had lined up an interview with him with the Washington Wizards. They were considering offering him a position on their recruiting team. I thought this was perfect. It was basketball that he loved, a good paying job, and there was travel involved, so maybe keeping him busy and away from my family would turn out to be a good thing. I looked up Benjamin's number to call him to give him the good news about the interview.

David Jr.

Since Benjamin reappeared, I had been so stressed and worried about Jada finding out the truth, I had not had time to check in with my sidekick, Gina. Gina and I met when she came to my school to do a story on me. She was an aspiring writer and she currently worked for a local station writing mostly sports related stories. I loved Jada, but there was something about Gina that drew me in. From the first moment I laid eyes on her, I knew I had to have her. It really started as something very innocent, but quickly turned into much more. She knew I was married, and I knew she had a steady boyfriend. A few months back, she and her boyfriend actually broke up and we were able to spend a lot more time together. I missed having that freedom now. I was curious about why she had not called me lately, especially since I had left her several messages yesterday. I dialed her cell number, but it went straight to voice mail. I left another message asking her to call me as soon as possible.

Vince

Today was a big day for Gina and I. We were going to our first prenatal appointment. Based on our calculations we expected her to be about ten to twelve weeks pregnant. I was slowly warming up to the idea of being a father. I knew going to this appointment, to talk to the doctor was a big step, and Gina was very happy to have me here with her. I had agreed to take the week off and spend time with her finishing the wedding plans, and to attend this appointment with her. The wedding planning was coming along nicely. We actually had a date set, so I needed to call my boy Darien and let him know. The doctor came into the room and started the exam. He asked Gina questions about her last period and then he called the nurse in and they performed an ultrasound. They were easily able to find the heartbeat, which brought Gina to tears, and they estimated that she was actually approximately fourteen weeks pregnant, based on the size of the baby. I was a little surprised by this estimate, but Gina seemed very disturbed. She kept asking the doctor to measure again to confirm the approximate due date. I just assumed she was worried about being further along than she thought and was concerned she would be really showing by the time we had the wedding in six weeks. We walked in silence to the car and once we were inside, I asked, "Gina, if you're worried about showing for the wedding pictures we can move the date up if you want?"

She turned to me and smiled. She said, "No Vince, its okay we are sticking to our date. Doctors make mistakes all the time with these tests.

Gina

Things were moving along as planned. Vince and I were making good progress on our wedding plans. Today was our first prenatal appointment. I could not wait to hear the baby's heartbeat, and get confirmation on my due date. I had already calculated that I was just about ten weeks pregnant. When the doctor said fourteen weeks, I almost fell off the table. I could not be that far along, it didn't make sense. Vince and I were kind of going through a rough spell during that time, so we had not really been together. Fortunately, Vince had not picked up on that and I was hoping he didn't think about it anymore. I could not believe that I might actually be carrying David's child instead of Vince. This just could not be happening. All of the careful planning I had done to get Vince to marry me, there was no way I was going to let this put a wrinkle in my plans. David was an okay guy, but my heart belonged to Vince and That's who I was going to marry. David was already married so there was no chance of him marrying me, anyway. In fact, one of the first things I needed to do when I get a spare moment away from Vince was to call David and officially break things off with him. I was not expecting any real drama from him. We both knew we were just having fun from the very beginning. Of course, I would not tell him about the baby, so there would be no reason for him to latch, on and try to make any trouble for me.

Chapter 17

Jada

Toni left the office immediately. I told her I would finish what I had to and then head over to her house. She was very upset about the most recent turn of events, understandably so. We had to talk and come up with a game plan for how to handle this one. One part of me was happy because surely a pregnancy by someone else, would keep Benjamin away. I thought about calling David to share the good news with him, but then thought better of it. Even after all this time, he still seemed to have a soft spot for Benjamin, and this is something that would definitely not go over well with him.

Toni

I do not even really remember driving home from the office, but next thing I knew I was sitting in my garage. I stayed in the car for a long time just sitting and thinking about everything. I kept replaying in my mind how this could have happened. I mean we had always been so careful. Then I thought about how well things had been going for us lately, and knew that that this would put a damper on my relationship plans. I knew Darien was going to feel like I purposely tried to trap him. I knew I wanted kids, but thought about if I really wanted one this way, possibly as a single mother. I finally decided to get out of the car and head into the house. I knew Jada was going to be arriving shortly and I had made a decision to tell her the truth about my internship. She had to know that to understand the impact this pregnancy was having on me. I knew it was going to be difficult to get through all of it without breaking down. I decided to try to write her a letter explaining everything, so I could just hand it to her and then once she read it we could talk. I knew there was no way I could get through any of it without breaking down. I was just finishing the letter when Jada arrived. I decided to type it because it would be faster than writing. When Jada walked in, I said, "Jada, I've mentioned to you a few times over the past few weeks that there are some things I need to tell Benjamin about which is why I have to see him now that he is back."

She nodded her head as she made herself comfortable on my couch. I continued, "Well, I need to share something with you, now that no one else in the entire world knows about my last year in college."

Jada looked very concerned and she stood up, walked over to me, and said, "Toni, whatever it's you can tell me, it will be okay."

The tears started flowing from my eyes and I reached into my pocket and pulled out the letter. I said through sniffles, "Jada I wrote you a letter explaining everything because I knew I would never get through all of it if I tried to tell you".

Jada looked at me and slowly reached towards the letter. She took it from my hand and then she started walking slowly back towards the couch. She kept looking at me and then the letter I handed her. When she sat down, she slowly unfolded it and looked at me one last time before she started reading the letter.

Dear Jada,

I'm very sorry that this is how You're finding out about all of this. Please do not feel like you're not my best friend because I kept this secret from you for so long. I felt I had to, in order for you to have peace and happiness with David. I never wanted to burden you with my troubles when I knew you had your own to deal with. I always felt you were suspicious about my internship during our senior year. It came up so suddenly, and I left, and didn't even come back to visit at all. Well the truth is that I was pregnant. I was pregnant and I was not sure who the father was. I didn't want to cause Benjamin any pain or grief when I knew all the pressure he was under to take the school to the finals, and worrying about the NBA draft. When I decided to leave to go to Chicago, it was to allow myself some time to think about my situation and make a decision about how to handle it. My plan was to stay away, have my baby, and then after the season and draft was over, talk to Benjamin and allow him to make a decision about what he wanted to do. When I found out that he had gotten injured and was told he would never play again, I wanted to come to him and tell him right then and there what was going on, but when I contacted you, you said he needed some time to deal with all of this and he would be in touch. I waited to hear from him for three months. I never heard anything. I decided to put the baby up for adoption and since I really was not sure who the father was, I was able to move forward without the fathers consent.

I'm sure now you can understand why I must talk to Benjamin, and maybe you will have a better understanding about why I'm going to do some of the things I plan to about this situation I'm in now with Darien. I hope you're not too upset with me for keeping this all from you, all of this time, but I really didn't want to put any more stress or pressure on you. You were already pregnant and you and David were trying to make plans for your lives together. Please forgive me.

Love T-

Jada

As I read the letter, I started to cry. By the time I was finished I was sobbing uncontrollably. Toni seemed perplexed by my reaction, and I almost thought, she thought I was angry with her. She walked over to me, gave me a box of tissues, and then sat down beside me on the couch. We sat there not saying a word to each other for a while. Both of us just crying and staring off into space. Finally, I turned to Toni and I said, "Toni, I'm so sorry that you had to go through all of that alone. I really wish you had confided in me sooner, but I do understand why you didn't."

Toni was still crying, but she nodded her head acknowledging what I had said. I rubbed my eyes and took a deep breath. Then I turned to her and said, "Toni, I've a secret I've been keeping from you as well". I hesitated for a moment before I continued, and Toni shifted in her seat. She seemed nervous about what I was going to say. After taking a few deep breaths, to get my courage up, I finally let out a heavy sigh and said, "Toni, I knew where Benjamin was all this time."

I stopped before I continued, to look at Toni, to gauge her reaction to that part of the news. She was shaking her head and mouthing the word, no. Her fist were clenched and she started pounding them on her knees. She looked at me and said, "Jada, you cannot be serious. You mean to tell me after all these years, after all the late nights, where I literally cried on your shoulder about Benjamin, you knew where he was and didn't tell me?"

Without even thinking, I simply responded, "Yes." The next thing I knew I felt a slap across my face. My immediate instinct was the fight back, but I knew deep down I deserved that one. I waited a minute for Toni to collect herself before I asked, "Can I continue?   There is more."

The hurt and anger in Toni's eyes cut right through my heart. Never in a million years had I wanted to see her so upset and hurt. She didn't say anything, but I could tell she was ready for me to continue. I thought very carefully how to tell Toni all of it, and I decided to tell her exactly how I found out about it all. I was hoping by doing it this way she would not feel like I had anything to do with the deception.

I got up and started pacing across the room. Eventually I said, "Toni, Benjamin has been in jail for the past seven years."

She jumped up and said, "In jail!! For what?"

"Toni calm down. Remember you're with child and don't need to allow yourself to get upset."

She sat back down and I started again, "Benjamin was in jail for the rape and attempted murder of a young girl."

She jumped up again and came at me like she wanted to choke me. She was screaming, "Jada you're such a liar. How could you lie to me about something like this? You knew how much I loved Benjamin. How could you keep this from me?"

I let her finish her tirade before I said, "Toni, it's the truth. Benjamin didn't get hurt during practice. He was arrested and was in jail. He and David went to a basketball team party one night, and somehow Benjamin ended up with some girl. He says the sex was consensual, but she cried rape, and he beat her so bad she was in a coma for a month."

Toni was sobbing and shaking her head and then she said, "Jada, I'm sorry, but I know Benjamin and this just cannot be true. Was there a trial or anything?" She asked.

"No there was no trial. David Sr.'s law firm represented Benjamin and he pleaded guilty to a lesser charge and was given the least amount of prison time possible."

Toni was still shaking her head and she said, "Jada, I'm telling you that there is more to this story. Are you sure you're telling me everything?"

Now I was nodding as I responded, "Yes Toni. I've told you everything I know."

Toni stood up and starting pacing back and forth and said, "Well I know there has to be more to this story. I'm going to call Benjamin to find out the truth from him. What you're telling me is just not adding up."

As soon as Toni mentioned calling Benjamin I started to panic. I completely forgot about the fact that David had made me promise not to tell Toni, unless I spoke to him first. Now my thoughts were focused on getting in touch with him to let him know I had spilled the beans. I had to convince Toni to wait before she called Benjamin. I needed some time to talk to David first.

"Toni," I said. "You're very upset and have a lot going on right now. You just found out you're pregnant by Darien and now you find out that Benjamin was in jail all this time. I think you need to take some time to digest everything before you call Benjamin."

Toni didn't respond right away. She just stared out the window and then she turned to me and said, "Jada I appreciate everything you have ever done for me, but right now I need to take control of my life. I agree, I need some time to think and digest everything, but I cannot promise you how long I can or will wait before I contact Benjamin. I would like some time alone now, if you do not mind. I need to write to collect my thoughts. I will give you a call later okay?"

I was torn. Part of me wanted to leave to go talk to David, and the other, wanted to stay and give my friend the support I knew she needed right now. I could tell by the look in her eyes she was serious. She needed some alone time, so I decided to let her alone at least for now. I let out a heavy sigh and said, "Okay Toni. I will leave you alone for now, but please call me in a few hours to let me know how you're doing. Okay?" She simply nodded her head as she walked toward the door to open it for me. I stopped to give her a hug as I walked out of the door.

As soon as I was in the car, I called David on his cell. He didn't answer, so I left him a message to call me right away. It was barely lunchtime, but I decided I needed some alone time and headed towards my house.

Toni

Journal Entry
Monday

I wish I knew where to start. There are so many emotions running through me right now none of this is probably going to make sense. First of all, I found out today that I'm pregnant. The good news is that this time, I know who the father is. There is only one possibility and that's Darien. The bad news is that I'm probably going to end up losing Darien, and being a single mother. I know I cannot give this child up. There is no way I can go through that pain again. The other news is that Jada finally came clean about knowing where Benjamin has been all of these years. Supposedly, he has been in jail. I mean, I guess it makes sense because I could never understand how he could just walk away from me like that. The love and bond we had was very strong. There was like a magnetic force pulling us towards one another, always. The part that's so hard to believe is that Jada said he was in jail for rape and attempted murder. Benjamin is not in the least bit a violent person, so that part of her story I cannot believe. Jada decided to tell me all of this after I told her about me being pregnant and giving the baby up. Right now, I'm so confused, lost, and hurt. I do not know which direction to go in. Part of me wants to reach out to Darien and tell him about our child, but I know his reaction will not be positive. The other part of me wants to call Benjamin and get his side of the story about this jail thing. Jada wanted me to wait before I contacted Benjamin, but I want answers and I want them now.

I got up from the bed where I had been writing and found the piece of paper with his number on it. I dialed the number, but it went straight to voice mail. I left him a message to call me right away. After all, of this excitement, I was a little hungry, so I went to fix myself something to eat and wait for Benjamin's return call.

Benjamin

David Sr. had called earlier to let me know he had arranged an interview for me with the Washington Wizards. I was very excited about it. I was starting to think he was not going to come through. I just wish he had given me a little more notice, but I was sitting in the lobby waiting for the person I was supposed to be speaking to. I had remembered to turn my phone off so there would be no distractions. I hoped that this interview went well. I was very anxious to get back in touch with Toni to let her know where I was, and I was hopeful that she would forgive me for leaving her like I did. My thoughts were interrupted by the receptionist calling my name. I stood up and headed towards the door to the conference room for my interview.

David Jr.

When I got out of my staff meeting, I turned on my phone and checked my messages. I had a message from Jada. I was hoping that Gina had called me back, but nothing from her yet. Jada's message sounded urgent so I called her right away. She answered immediately.

"David, I told Toni about Benjamin."

I could not believe my ears. I shifted the phone to my other ear and said, "What are you talking about Jada?"

"It's kind of a long story, but the bottom line is that I told her that Benjamin was in jail for the last seven years."

I let out a heavy sigh and said, "Jada why in the hell did you do that? We agreed. How did she react? Did she call Benjamin?" I was firing questions at her so fast she didn't have time to answer. Finally, I took and breath and she said, "David, she doesn't believe me. She said she wanted to call Benjamin to get his side of the story. I convinced her to wait a little bit, so I would have time to talk to you."

Okay, Jada well I need to try to get in touch with Benjamin before she does. Let me try to reach him and I will call you back." I hung up before she could respond. I immediately dialed Benjamin's number and it went straight to voice mail. I left a message for him to call me right away. I also sent him a text message in case he read those first. My message said, *Benjamin 911 Toni knows call me right away.* As soon as I sent the text to Benjamin, my phone rang and I answered without looking the caller ID.

"Benjamin?"

"Um no this is Gina, David. Who is Benjamin?"

I was caught off guard by Gina's voice because I was expecting Benjamin. I had to regroup. Finally, I said, "Oh, hey, Gina. I was expecting a call from my boy Benjamin."

"Oh, I see," she said.

"So what's been going on with you? I've not heard from you in a while."

She responded, "Well actually, I've been a little under the weather and I have news."

I wanted to cut this call short so I said, "Oh, what's the news, did you finally get that promotion you've been after or something?"

She chuckled and said, "No actually the news is that I'm getting married."

This caught me off guard. I said, "Oh, wow, that's a shock. I thought things were not going so well for you two lately?"

She said, "Yeah, well things have a way of working themselves out. So anyway I just wanted to let you know that and I won't be seeing you anymore."

I was trying not to react negatively, but my pride was hurt. I was not in love with Gina by any means, but for a man it's always better if a relationship ends on our terms, not theirs. I finally said, "Okay Gina. Well if that's how you want it, that's fine. I mean we both knew going into this that we were both attached. I wish you and Vince luck on your marriage and I do hope you get that promotion, you deserve it."

She sighed and said, "Thanks David. I really appreciate you not causing any drama about this. You're a great guy and it was a pleasure getting to know you."

I simply said, "take care Gina", and ended the call. I could not believe that Gina dumped me. I was sure that she was in love with me, and that things were not working out with she and Vince. I guess I read that wrong. I had other more pressing issues to deal with right now. I would give it a few days and then call her back to press for details on the sudden change of heart.

Chapter 18

Benjamin

My interview went very well. They offered me my dream job on the spot. Well actually, the dream job would be a starting position or head coach, but under the circumstances, being a recruiter was as good as it gets. The starting salary was a lot more than I expected. This was exactly what I needed to get myself back on my feet and make a life for Toni and I. I could not wait to call Toni, but I promised David Sr. I would be in contact with him first. As I walked to my car, I turned on my phone. I had a few voice mails and a text message. I read the text message first. It was from David Jr. I almost dropped the phone. Oh my gosh, Toni knew. I jumped in my car and started driving towards Pennsylvania. I didn't even check the voice mails. I knew one of them if not both were from Toni.

I called David back. He answered immediately, "Benjamin, I'm sorry, but Jada told Toni everything, well not everything, but you know what I mean. Now what are we going to do?"

I said, "David I'm on my way up there now. I have another message on my phone that I'm sure is from Toni. I'm coming up there to talk to her in person. I do not want to do this over the phone."

David Jr. said, "Okay well why don't I meet you at Toni's house in about two hours."

I looked at my watch and said, "Make it an hour and a half, traffic is moving along well. I'm only a few miles away from 695 now."

David Jr. said, "Okay I will meet you there."

I decided to listen to my messages. I was right the first one was from Toni, and she sounded upset, but not as bad as I expected. She asked me to call her right away. The next message was from David Jr. I thought about calling Toni back, but decided to wait until I was much closer, so she would not have time to leave. I needed to talk to her face to face. Today was going to be a great day. I got the job of my dreams and I was going to get my woman. What more could a man ask for?

David Jr.

I had an hour and a half to figure out how I was going to handle this situation with Jada. I thought about going home, but didn't want to run into Jada right now. Then I would have to explain why I was going back out. No, right now the best thing for me to do was lay low and wait for Benjamin to arrive. I decided to stop and get a quick bite to eat. I could kill some time that way. I pulled into the parking lot of the diner and sat in my car for a few minutes. I needed some quiet meditation time. I replayed everything in my head about that night so many years ago, when I completely lost it and changed my life and the life of my best friend, forever. Benjamin really was the best friend I had in the entire world, next to Jada of course. I thought about how the truth would hurt her. I thought about how bad it would be if she found out about Gina. My infidelity is something I was not proud of, at all. I really loved Jada and she was a wonderful wife and mother to our children. I could not come up with a good reason for me being unfaithful. We had a healthy sex life and Jada took really good care of herself and me. She damned near worshiped me. We tried to do the right thing by attending church regularly and exposing our children to religion. I had taken those vows, and I really meant them when I did, but something always pulled me away from her and led me astray. I decided that if I was able to prevent her from finding out the truth about Benjamin taking the blame for me, I was going to break things off with Gina for good and concentrate on rebuilding my marriage. I decided no more extra marital affairs. Jada was a great woman and I needed to appreciate her and be more respectful of her and our marriage.

I briefly thought about how disappointed my father would be if he knew I was still sleeping around on Jada. After the incident, he gave me a very stern talking to about how serious wedding vows were, and told me if I was not ready to be committed, not to do it. At the time, I thought I was committed and would be able to be faithful to Jada. I made it about a year into our marriage before I started meeting other women and having affairs. It was very easy because I was around the schools, and single desperate woman were everywhere. The only problem is they were always looking for a husband and I was already married. Usually once, they discovered that the relationship didn't last long. Gina had been different because she was not desperate and she was not a single mother. I cannot explain it, but we just hit it off right from the beginning.

My cell phone rang and interrupted my thoughts. I looked at the caller ID and saw that it was Jada. I answered.

"Hey babe, what's going on?"

"David, where are you?" Jada asked sounding very upset.

I responded, "Babe what's wrong?"

"David, please just answer me. Where are you?"

I switched the phone to my other ear and said, "Jada, I'm on my way to a meeting, what is going on?"

"I need you to meet me at the hospital right away. Tre fell off the monkey bars at school and he broke his arm. The nurse said it's a compound fracture and he's going to need surgery."

I threw the car in reverse and said, "Oh my God Jada, which hospital?"

Jada sniffled and said, "They're taking him to the pediatric trauma unit."

I thought for a minute to try to get my bearing on the fastest way to get there.

"Okay babe. I will meet you there in about 10 – 15 minutes."

Jada responded, "okay honey I'm on my way too. I'll see you there."

I made my way out of the parking lot and headed towards the interstate. That was going to be the quickest route to the hospital. I know I was driving too fast, but I had to get their as soon as possible. The on-ramp to the interstate was a little backed up as usual. Some cars were hanging back halfway up the ramp so that they could pick up enough speed to merge into traffic. I always hated this on-ramp it was very dangerous. When it was my turn, I checked for traffic and I sped up to make my way onto the highway. I never saw the truck switching lanes until it was too late.

Jada

I arrived at the hospital ahead of the ambulance that was carrying Tre. I've no clue how that happened. I must have been doing 100 miles an hour, or something. As soon as the ambulance pulled up, I ran out to meet them. Tre was in so much pain. I could hear his screams as soon as they opened the doors. I immediately started to cry. They rushed him in and started working on him. One of the nurses pulled me aside and told me to start filling out the necessary paperwork. It only took about fifteen minutes for a doctor to come out to talk to me. I kept looking around for David. He should have been here by now. What was going on? I had turned my cell phone off when I came into the emergency room. The doctor said they were prepping Tre for surgery and were about to take him up in about ten minutes. He asked me if I was going to go up with him, or wait for my husband. I told him I was not sure I was going to go outside and call my husband to see where he was.

I stepped outside and turned on my phone. I dialed David's number and it rang, but he didn't pick up. I started to leave a message but decided to hang up and try again. I tried again and still no answer. I had no idea where he was, but I was going to go back in, and go up with Tre. I turned my phone back off and went back into the hospital. They were just about to wheel Tre up for surgery. He had been sedated, so he barely knew I was there, even though I was holding his hand. I knew David was on his way, so I asked one of the nurses to send him upstairs when he arrived. She assured me she would and we headed up to the surgical floor. Once we got there, of course, I had to let go of Tre's hand and I had to go to the waiting room to wait. The doctor said it could be a few hours. The compound fracture was pretty bad, and he tried to explain to me everything they were going to have to do, but I really was not paying attention. My mind kept wandering to David and wondering where he was. As the minutes passed, I became more and more concerned. I kept wondering where David was and I finally decided to try to call him again. Again, no answer this time, straight to voice mail, which I thought, was a good sign. That must mean he has entered the hospital and will be here shortly. Just as I was, about to turn off my cell phone it rang and it was a number I didn't recognize. I answered.

"Hello".

The voice on the other end was a stranger and they said, "Is this Mrs. David Wright?"

I tried to place the voice. It sounded vaguely familiar, but I could not figure out why. I responded, "Yes this is Mrs. Wright, how can I help you?"

The strange woman said, "Oh my goodness." and the call ended.

I pulled the phone from my ear, stared at it for a moment, and thought to myself that was strange. I tried to call the number back and it went to the hospital operator. Okay now that was really odd. I hung up and got up. Just as I did, I saw the nurse from downstairs walking towards me with a look of concern on her face. My hands immediately went to my chest.

"Oh no, what's wrong with my baby?" I asked.

She was shaking her head, then said, "No ma'am it's not your son. It's your..."

She paused and swallowed hard and took a breath. Then she said, "It's your husband. He's been in a terrible accident and he was just brought into the emergency room downstairs." I felt lightheaded and dizzy. She anticipated this and grabbed my arm to steady me. She said, "Why don't you sit down? Is there anyone you can call to come be with you?"

Immediately, I thought about Toni. I knew she was very upset, but I needed her right now. "Yes," I answered. "I can call my friend and she can come."

The nurse said, "Give me her name, and number and I will make the call for you."

I nodded my head and asked, "is my husband going to be okay?" She didn't respond right away and the look in her eyes said it all. I knew David was not going to be okay.

Toni

I hung up the phone, and grabbed my keys and my purse to head to the hospital. The nurse I spoke to didn't give me a lot of information, but I knew that Jada needed me. Both Tre and David were at the hospital and they were both in bad shape. I had no idea what had happened, but the nurse told me to get there right away and to be careful.. I opened the door and saw a man walking towards my house. At first, I didn't recognize him until he was standing right in front of me. I stopped dead in my tracks and said, "Benjamin, is that you?"

He looked the same, but very different at the same time. He answered, "Yes, Toni, it's me."

I threw my hands up and said, "Benjamin I don't have time for any drama today. Jada explained everything to me, but I know there is more to this story."

He interrupted me and said, "Yes Toni there is that's why I'm here."

I continued past him and said in passing, "Well we are going to have to talk about all of this later. I'm on my way to the hospital. David and Tre are there and they're both hurt real bad."

Benjamin started to walk towards me and said, "What happened?"

I stopped long enough to turn around and say, "I don't know."

He said, "Let me drive you."

I thought for a minute then said, "No Benjamin I really don't want to be alone with you right now. If you want to come you can follow me."

He hung his head and said, "Okay Toni, lead the way. I will follow."

When we arrived at the hospital, we both parked in the emergency area and headed inside. The nurse told me where to meet her and Jada. As I approached the door, a nurse was standing there and she asked me if I was Toni. Once I confirmed who I was, she filled me in on what she knew. Tre had fallen off the monkey bars at school and had a nasty break. He was in surgery and it was going well. David was on his way to the hospital and was in a terrible accident. He was dead on arrival to the hospital. The nurse said his injuries were way too extensive. In his haste to get to the hospital, he had pulled into the path of a tractor-trailer on the interstate. Jada didn't know yet. They were waiting for me to arrive to break the news to her. When we walked into the room, Jada was a complete mess. I ran to her and embraced her. Once she realized I wasn't alone she pushed me away and said, "What is he doing here?"

I grabbed her again and started hugging her again. I whispered in her ear, "Don't worry about that right now."

Jada pulled away from me again and started, "Toni, Tre got hurt at school and then David."

I put my finger to her lips and said, "Jada, I already know honey. The nurse explained everything to me."

She continued, "But they won't tell me anything about David. They just said he was in a car accident, but nothing else."

Just then, the door opened and a doctor walked in. Jada leapt at him and said, "Please tell me what's going on with my son... and my husband."

The doctor motioned for us to all sit down. I sat next to Jada and held her hand. I knew what was coming, but tried to remain calm and keep my emotions in check. The doctor started with an update on Tre. "His surgery was finished and he is in recovery. Everything went well and you can see him as soon as you feel you're ready."

Jada looked confused and said, "Why wouldn't I be ready to see him now? I don't understand."

The doctor cleared his throat then continued, "Mrs. Wright...about your husband... well ma'am, I'm sorry, but we did everything we could, but his injuries were too severe and we were unable to revive him."

As soon as he said, I'm sorry, Jada grabbed onto me and starting sobbing uncontrollably. She screamed, "No, No, No, not my David. Lord please, not my David."

The doctor stood up to leave, and I nodded to him it was okay for him to leave us alone.

It took almost an hour for Benjamin and I to get Jada calm enough to leave the room we were in. Benjamin excused himself at one point and went to call David Sr. to break the news to him. I didn't know what to do, or what to say to Jada. She was always the one taking care of me and comforting me. Nothing bad ever happened to her. One of the nurses came into check on us, and sat with Jada while I went into to check on Tre. Jada was in no condition to see him, and I didn't want him to feel alone. What I was not prepared for was his questions about where his mommy and daddy were. As soon as he asked me, my tears started flowing. I tried to regain my composure then said, "Tre, honey, your mommy is going to be here soon to talk to you. She's a little upset right now."

Luckily, he was still a little drowsy from the anesthesia, so he didn't press the issue. He just closed his eyes and dosed back off to sleep.

Chapter 19

Benjamin

Toni and I really had a hard time with Jada. I decided to make the phone call to David Sr. I was concerned about his safety also, so I only told him that David had been in an accident and was hurt pretty bad. I also mentioned that Tre had fallen and broke his arm. He said he was calling for his car and would be there within two hours. Toni was keeping her distance from me, but I caught her looking at me a few times when she thought I was not looking. I'm sure me showing up like this was a big shock to her. I knew what I initially came here to do, but now all bets were off because I could not expose David's past in the middle of all of this. For now, I knew that things would have to stay as they have been. At least Toni knew that I had been in jail and not with another woman. I knew that both Jada and David Sr. were going to need a lot of support and I was going to focus on doing whatever I could to help them through this difficult trying time. I told Toni to take Jada home after they stopped in to check on Tre. I was going to wait at the hospital for Senior to arrive. I would handle him, and we thought he might be better able to talk to Tre. Toni and Jada were going to head home to talk to Jada's daughter Jayden.

Darien

I had tried to reach Toni several times today. She was not online at work today either. I had tried her cell phone several times this evening, and it kept going straight to voice mail. I was getting concerned about her. The last time I called, I left her a message letting her know that I was thinking about her and was concerned that I had not been able to reach her.

Gina

Vince and I had a full day, we had just gotten back to the house, and he turned on the TV. There was a story on about a big accident on the interstate today involving a tractor-trailer and one person was killed. They said David Wright, and I turned around just in time to see a picture of David on the screen. I screamed, "Oh my God!"

Vince jumped out of his chair, ran over to me, and said, "What's wrong baby? Are you in pain?"

I pushed him away and said, "No. I know that guy. I did a story on him last year."

Vince said, "Oh baby please don't scare me like that again."

I had to contact the station to get more information on exactly what happened. I grabbed my cell phone and called my favorite contact that always had the scoop. I wanted to find out who was going to do the story and interview the family. I needed to know more about the family; in case this was, in fact, David's child I was carrying.

Toni

After Jada and I left the hospital, I stopped by my house quick to grab some clothes. I was going to stay with her tonight. I knew she shouldn't be alone.. The talk with Jayden went pretty well. She is so young she understood that Daddy was hurt real bad and not coming back, but beyond that, I'm not real sure what she understood. Jada appeared to be walking around in a daze. She was completely emotionless. I felt like she had cried all of her tears out and there simply was not anything left. It was almost eleven p.m. before I got Jada and Jayden both settled down for the night. I was exhausted physically, and mentally, myself. I was just getting a chance to turn on my cell phone. I had several messages. I checked them and they were from Darien and Benjamin. I really didn't have the energy to deal with either of them right now, but I knew that at the very least I needed to return Darien's calls. He said in his last message he was concerned. I checked the time again and decided to try to catch him before he turned in for the night. I dialed his number, he answered on the third ring, and he sounded half-asleep. I said, "Darien, I'm sorry to call you so late."

He said, "No problem Toni, what's going on? I've been trying to reach you all day. I was getting worried about you."

I was fighting back tears. Through all of this with David, I had not really allowed myself to let go and really grieve. I took a deep breath and said, "Yes, well, it's been a really tough day. My best friend's son got hurt at school. He fell off the monkey bars and broke his arm really bad. It was a compound fracture and required surgery."

"Wow, Toni that's terrible," Darien said.

171

I continued, "Well that's not the worse part about it. Her husband was rushing to the hospital to meet her and was in a terrible accident and was killed."

"Oh my," Darien said. "That's terrible Toni. How is she doing? I mean obviously she's been through a lot today."

Through tears, I said, "Yes, it's been a very tough day for everyone. I'm staying with her to help her with the arrangements and her kids."

"Is there anything I can do Toni?" Darien asked. I thought for a minute about my own little personal issue that I would need to deal with at some point with Darien. I didn't want to discuss it tonight and didn't want to do it over the phone.

I said, "Well I do need to see you. Are you coming home this weekend?"

"Well, I wasn't planning on it, but I certainly can make plans to be there this weekend if you need me," Darien said.

I smiled and said, "Yes Darien I really need to see you this weekend. At this point I'm not sure when the services for David will be, but I need to see you this weekend."

"No problem baby. I will be there on Friday. If you need anything before then, or just need to talk to someone call me anytime. Okay?" Darien said.

I was still smiling through my tears and I said, "Thanks Darien that means a lot to me. I will be in touch with you once I find out about the arrangements. Good night."

I decided I would deal with Benjamin tomorrow. I plugged my cell phone in to charge it and grabbed my journal to start writing. I needed to clear my head before I tried to get some sleep. I knew tomorrow and the next few days were going to be very hectic and emotionally draining for me.

Journal Entry
Monday Night

Today is one of those days where I sit back and reflect on my life. It's so easy to complain about your life and all that's going wrong or missing in it. Then something happens to someone else. It makes you thankful that it was not you. You also feel bad about all the complaining you were doing about your problems. Earlier today, I found out, I was pregnant by someone I'm just getting to know. I was devastated and my best friend Jada was by my side trying to help me make sense of it and decide how to move forward. I feel guilty now for some of the thoughts I had then. I was thinking about how perfect Jada's life seemed to me. She was married to the love of her life, her high school sweetheart. They have two beautiful children and a wonderful life together. I've always envied her life. Now her life has been completely ripped apart. Her husband was killed today in a terrible accident. In an instant, she is a single mother, a widow. David was the only man she has ever been with. He was her entire world aside from the kids.

She has always been there for me through all of my trials and tribulations, so now that she needs me, I'm not real sure what to do. Thank goodness, her family is coming tomorrow to help with the arrangements. She has not been real close to them since she married David. Her mother and father didn't really approve of their marriage, since David was white, but under the circumstances, they're putting all of that aside to support their daughter. Jada's mother was a real take-charge kind of person, so I knew she would make sure everything was handled, but then again

David Sr. was also very controlling, so this could be very interesting. I was going to take the rest of the week off to help with whatever I could, and I needed some me time to get my mind together to deal with both Benjamin and Darien.

After today, I've decided that I'm going to go ahead with this pregnancy, with or without Darien. Life is too short and this might be my only opportunity to have a child. I know I want one and now is as good a time as any. When I see Darien this weekend, I am going to be straight with him.. Tell him I'm pregnant and it's his child. Let him know that I would love for him to be a part of my life and the baby's life, but if he decides he doesn't want to that's fine, I will handle it on my own. I'm not going to press the issue about a relationship for us because I know he will feel like I was trying to trap him.

I still wanted to let Benjamin know about the pregnancy, seven years ago, and I wanted to hear his side of the story regarding his time in jail, but at this point, I was over him. I never thought I would be able to say it and mean it but I'm officially over Benjamin. Seeing him today for the first time in over seven years was good. He looked great but I realized that all of these feelings are in the past. I will always love him and he will always be special to me, but I cannot see myself just jumping back into a relationship with him. The reality is that I've changed and grown a lot over the past seven years. I'm sure he has too, so we cannot just pick up where we left off. It's really just not that simple. I really hope that Benjamin understands that and does not have any thoughts about us being back together again.

Benjamin

I was finally settled into my hotel room and trying to make sense of everything that had happened today. David

Sr. took the news a lot better than I expected, in fact, I think he is in shock and it really has not set in yet. We both talked to Tre. Although he didn't know me, he seemed comfortable with me, as soon as his grandfather told him I was a good friend of his father's from school. Tre took the news pretty hard. He cried for a long time, which is understandable. He was only seven and this was his first experience with death. He still has to heal from his own injuries and they have him under slight sedation tonight. They feel he will come home in another couple of days, which should be in time for him to attend the services for his father.

David Sr. didn't mention anything about Toni. I guess now that David was gone it didn't matter to him if Jada found out the truth or not. It mattered to me that Toni knew the truth, and under the circumstances, I was more confident than ever that Toni would keep the truth from Jada. The only problem was that I could not be sure that Toni would believe me and without David to verify my story, I would be like every other convict who swore it was not them. I just knew that I was prepared to do whatever I needed to do, to get Toni back. She was the love of my life. I never wanted anyone else. The only thing that kept me going those seven years in prison was knowing that she was out here, waiting for me. The only problem was she was not waiting for me because she never got the letters I wrote to her and sent through David. I loved my boy, but I was still angry at him for that. It was very selfish of him to keep those from her.

Suddenly it occurred to me that maybe Toni was with someone else now, and it would not be that simple for me to walk back into her life. This is not something I had considered before. There was something about the way she looked at me today; it was so cold and hard, like she was finished with me. It really bothered me how Jada reacted to seeing me also. Clearly, she views me as a monster because of what David told her about what happened. It's ironic because she was actually sleeping next to the monster she feared for the past seven years. At this point, all I could do was tell Toni the truth and see where she wanted things to go from there. I decided to let her reach out to me. I knew that she was going to be dealing with a lot, trying to be there for Jada. I was not going to push the issue. After the funeral for David, I was going to go back to Maryland and focus on my new job. No matter what happened with Toni I needed a fresh new start, and this job was exactly what I needed.

Chapter 20

Friday
Toni

The service for David was very nice. Jada's mom and David Sr. were able to work together and put together a very nice service for him. Jada and the kids made it through all right. Tre broke down towards the end, but he is also still in a lot of physical pain from his surgery. He was just released from the hospital late yesterday afternoon and faces several months of therapy. Benjamin of course did the eulogy. It was very touching to hear him express his affection for David even though it had been so long since they had seen each other. I noticed how David Sr. kept a close eye on him the entire time. Almost like he was hanging on every word that he said. Jada put up a little bit of resistance about Benjamin saying anything at the service. She was harboring a lot of hostility and resentment about his imprisonment. She kept saying she didn't want to be associated with a rapist and murderer. Every time she said those words, I shuttered at the thought of them being used to describe Benjamin. I knew in the core of my being that he had not done what he was accused of. One day, I would get to the bottom of the truth.

I was very surprised at the number of local people who showed up for the service. A lot of women, which made me raise my eyebrow, but no one else seemed to notice. I guess it made sense because of all of the teams David had worked with over the years. I assumed these were the mothers of his kids he worked with. There was one woman in particular who caught my eye. She looked familiar, but I could not place her right away. She seemed especially interested in Jada and the family, as she watched them the entire time. She obviously was not close enough to the family to approach them to talk, because she kept her distance. When we left the church, there was a news van outside, and immediately I remembered where I had seen the woman before. She was the reporter who had done a story on David about a year ago. That explained her interest. She was probably digging for some dirt to do another story or something. I also noticed that she approached Benjamin to talk to him after we went outside. I was a little curious about that conversation, but not enough to approach Benjamin about it.

Darien was due home later this evening, but we didn't have any plans to see each other until tomorrow. I knew that I would be tied up and too emotionally exhausted to have that conversation with him. Benjamin had been great this week. He was around doing whatever was needed to help, but he didn't try to corner me to talk about anything, which was nice. I had not decided if I wanted to get my talk with him over with before I saw Darien or if I wanted to let some time pass before we opened up those wounds. I would see how things went for the rest of the day before I decided when I would talk to Benjamin.

Benjamin

I made it though the service without getting too emotional. David Sr. was right there hanging on every word when I did the eulogy. I actually think he thought I would mention something about the incident. I have no idea why he would think I would do something like that, but clearly he does not trust me. Jada was still tolerating me, but clearly didn't want me around. That made me sad because she had no idea how much David and she really meant to me. David was not the only reason that I took the blame, it was for her and their unborn child also.

Toni and I were spending a lot of time around each other, but had not made any moves towards talking about all the things that needed discussed. I was really hoping we would get a chance to talk today before I left. I really needed to get my side of the story out there. I needed to know if there was even a glimmer of hope that we could reconcile. A news reporter who wanted to interview me about my relationship with David interrupted my thoughts. She was inquiring about how I knew him. I took her card and told her I would consider talking to her sometime next week. Now was not the time.

Jada

The past few days have seemed like a blur. I still do not think that it has completely sunk in to me that David is gone. I'm numb. I cannot feel anything. My mother and Toni have been wonderful. Even David Sr. has been great. He has been a big help with Tre. He has offered to come up to stay with me to help with Tre until he is completely healed. I didn't accept his offer right away, although I probably will. I

179

could really use the help, but on the other hand having him around will be a constant reminder of David for me. I'm not sure I can handle that. My parents were great; they got along with David Sr., which was a relief. The last thing I needed was them fighting in the middle of all of this. Benjamin has been around much to my dismay. I really wish he would just go away. I'm not the least bit comfortable being near him and him being near my children. David Sr. seems a little uncomfortable with him being around also, but I figured I would allow him to do the eulogy since he was his closest friend.

I had no idea what I was going to do next. I was not worried about work right now. My boss came to the service to pay her respects. She had called me earlier in the week to tell me to take as much time as I needed to get myself together. Part of me wanted to just curl up in a ball and cry, and the fighter in me wanted answers, like why me? Who was at fault for the accident, David or the truck driver? I wondered if David would still be here if Tre had not gotten hurt. Some people say when it's your time to go; it's your time to go. So would he have been in an accident even if he had not been on his way to the hospital? What about all those women who were at the service, who were they? Why were they there? I recognized the reporter who had done the story on David before. She was there. I guess trying to get a new story. I also noticed her talking to Benjamin after the service. I had to ask Benjamin about that.

I know it's customary for close friends and family to gather after the services, but I was drained and just wanted to be alone. I explained this to my mother She said she would greet the guests, and tell everyone I was not feeling well and was lying down. She told me to take as much time as I needed. I lay awake staring at the ceiling for what felt like hours.. At some point, I drifted off to sleep because when I awoke the house was quiet. I gathered myself together to go downstairs to see what was going on. I found my parents, David Sr., Toni and Benjamin. I had slept through everything. All of the other guests were gone. I walked in and everyone stopped what they were doing to look at me.

I said, "Thanks to all of you for everything you have done to help me over the past few days. I really love and appreciate all of you. I don't know how I would have made it without you."

Toni was the first to make it to my side to give me a hug. My mom and dad were right behind her. David Sr. gave me the longest hug of all. It was like he didn't want to let me go. He whispered in my ear, "Jada if you or the kids ever need anything, do not hesitate to call me. You're all I've left in this world."

I pulled myself away from him and said, "Thanks David. I really appreciate that. I think we are both going to need each other."

Benjamin didn't approach me he just said, "Jada if you need anything just call me." I just nodded my head.

Everyone decided to leave me alone tonight. There had been someone with me every night this week, and it was time for me to have some time alone. The kids were already in bed, thanks to my mom. David Sr. was going to come back on Sunday night to help with Tre's therapy next week. I told him he didn't have to because I didn't have to go back to work yet, but he insisted. Toni was the first to head out, followed by Benjamin and David Sr. My mom fixed me a plate of food and then she and my dad left. I tried to eat, but really had no appetite. I sat at the table looking around at all of the stuff that meant absolutely nothing to me anymore without David to share it with.

Toni

As I walked to my car, I thought about the talk I needed to have with Benjamin; was now the right time or not? I decided that I did want to get this over with, so I could start with a fresh mind when I talked to Darien tomorrow. I turned and Benjamin was right behind me.

"Benjamin, I was just coming to find you. Would you like to go somewhere to talk?"

Without hesitating, he said, "Yes I would…where?"

I thought for a minute and said, "Why don't you just follow me back to my place? We really need to talk in private."

Benjamin smiled and said, "Ok, that sounds good."

I had to make sure he understood that nothing was going to happen between us so I said, "Benjamin we are just going to talk. Nothing else, I'm in a relationship right now."

I could tell he was disappointed but he said, "I understand, no problem."

Benjamin

I could not believe it. She was in a relationship, so what was the point of telling my side of the story now. I wanted her and since I could not have her. I was asking myself, was it even worth it to talk to her about everything?

Just as I was turning onto her street, my cell phone rang. I answered the call from David Sr., "Hello."

"Benjamin. What are you doing?"   David Sr. said. "I'm going to talk to Toni, sir."

He sighed heavily into the phone, and then said, "Benjamin what good is any of this going to do now? David is dead. Do you really want to bring all of this out now about him and his past?"

I thought for a minute and he was right. Was there any point? "Sir all this time my goal was to get back with Toni. I just found out that she is in a relationship with someone, so maybe there is no point, but I have to talk to her, sir. I'm sure that she will not say anything to Jada. She would not want to hurt her. There would be no point in hurting Jada anymore than she is already hurting."

He thought for a minute and said, "Yes I guess you're right. Well do what you feel you have to, but call me and let me know what happens."

I said "Okay" and ended the call. I sat in front of Toni's house wondering if I really wanted to go in and go through all of this if I knew she was not going to take me back. I finally decided that it meant more to me that she knew the truth, even if she didn't take me back. I got out of my car and walked towards her door. I rang the doorbell and Toni opened the door and said, "Come on in Benjamin. I've been waiting for you and waiting for this day."

Toni

When Benjamin arrived, I decided to get right to the point. We went into the living room and I offered him a drink before I got started. He declined. I sat down across from him and started, "Benjamin, before you tell me about why you were in prison. I need to tell you something very important."

He put his hand up and said, "Toni, I heard you loud and clear. You're in a relationship with someone else, so I know that we cannot be together right now."

"Yes, that's true, but that's not what I was going to say."

"Okay, so what else is there to say?"

I stood up and starting pacing and then said, "Benjamin I left to go to Chicago for that internship because I was pregnant."

He jumped up and said, "WHAT!!!!"

I put my hands up and said, "Benjamin please calm down and let me finish please."

He didn't say anything, but he sat down. I continued, "I got pregnant right after you and I had gotten back together, senior year. Remember we had broken up for a little while at the beginning of the year?"

He nodded yes, but didn't say anything. I continued, "Well while we were apart I met someone else and slept with him. I found out I was pregnant after you and I got back together. I really was not sure who the father was. You were doing so well and was expecting a NBA contract offer. I didn't want to be in your way, or cause you any problems. I decided to go away and have the baby."

He interrupted me again and said, "We have a baby?" I shook my head no and said, "Benjamin please let me get through all of this and then you can ask your questions. I went to Chicago to have the baby and my plan was to tell you about it after the baby was born. I wanted to have you and the other potential father tested, so we could determine who the father was, and then we could decide how to proceed with our relationship. Jada contacted me to let me know that you had gotten hurt, and I wanted to come to you then and tell you everything. She told me you needed some time and space and you would be in touch with me. I waited for three months and I never heard from you, so I put the baby up for adoption."

Benjamin was up on his feet now. He came towards me and grabbed my shoulders, "Toni, why didn't you tell me? Things could have been so different if you had just told me what was going on."

I stepped back from his grip and said, "Benjamin at the time I thought I was doing what was best for you. I didn't want to distract you with a baby, especially if it wasn't yours."

"What about the other guy?" he asked.

I shook my head and answered, "I was never able to locate him. He doesn't know either."

Benjamin sat back down and put his head in his hands. After a few minutes, he looked back up at me and his eyes were wet with tears. He said, "Toni is there anything else?"

I shook my head, no.

Benjamin stood up and I thought he was about to leave. He turned his back to me and then he said, "Toni I have to explain everything to you, but before I do, you have to promise me something."

"What's that Benjamin?"

"You have to promise me not to discuss any of this with Jada."

Now I was confused. Jada?" I asked, "What does she have to do with any of this?"

He motioned for me to sit down then he started, "Toni what I need to tell you has everything to do with Jada, because it's about her and David. Like you, I made certain decisions back then because I thought I was doing the right thing, but now it seems like all the wrong choices were made."

I had no idea what he was talking about, but I didn't say a word. I just sat and waited for him to continue.

"Jada told you I was in jail and she told you that I raped and tried to kill someone, right?" I nodded my head yes and he continued, "Well it wasn't me who did those things. It was David."

I could not react at first. I was thinking about everything and trying to piece it all together. I was not sure if I should or could trust Benjamin, but Jada didn't seem to have all of the answers when I asked so, she really didn't know what had happened either. She told me that what she knew she had been told by David, so maybe Benjamin was telling the truth. I said, "Benjamin please start from the beginning and tell me everything."

As Benjamin explained how they were at the party, everyone was drinking, and David ended up with some girl and had sex with her. Then she cried rape because she thought he was a future NBA star. David was drunk, lost it, and beat her within an inch of her life. He told me how he decided to take the blame instead of David because Jada was pregnant, and he didn't want their child to grow up without a father. I just started crying as the story unfolded. I could not believe the irony all around. Benjamin didn't want their child to be without a father when all the while it was possible that his child had been deprived of their father. I thought about how Jada could not stand Benjamin because he was a rapist when it was really David who had been with the girl. Not that he was a rapist, it seems like it was truly consensual sex, but still he cheated on her. I understood why Benjamin made me promise and based on what I was hearing, there was no way I was going to be the one to let Jada know about all of this. She didn't need this on top of the other pain she was already dealing with.

Benjamin explained that he wrote me several letters telling me everything so I would know where he was. He didn't want me to think he had abandoned me. David was supposed to send me the letters. Obviously, David never gave them to me. Benjamin said once he got out David told him that he never sent them, because he was worried that Jada would find out the truth. Benjamin was also very concerned about the child I gave up. He kept asking me questions that I could not answer. He wanted to know if I wanted to find the child, and see if we could determine if he was in fact the father. I didn't want to let him know that I was pregnant again. I simply told him to think about it and really, what damage it could do to the child, who would be seven years old now. He said he would think about it, but he really thought he wanted to pursue it with, or without, my help.

We talked for another hour, or so, and then he left. The entire conversation went much better than I expected and we parted ways both knowing that what we had in the past, was in the past. He tried to bring up my current relationship, but I told him I would not discuss it with him. He told me about his job that David Sr. had helped him get, and he was very excited about that. He said he would be in touch with me if he decided to pursue finding the child I gave up. As the potential father, he thought he might have some rights since he was never given a chance to give up his rights in the first place.

Journal Entry
Friday night
    It was a long, emotionally draining week. I finally talked to Benjamin and we both had bombshells to drop. He told me that he took the blame for David's crime. I told him about the baby. If we had both been honest with each other, back then things could have been very different. If Benjamin had known about the baby, he would never have agreed to take the blame for David's crime. I wondered how they had gotten the girl that was involved, to go along with their story. Surely, she knew it was David, and not Benjamin. David was white and Benjamin is black. Benjamin mentioned that David Sr. was involved, and I imagined he had something to do with keeping the girl and everyone else quiet. I was glad this was behind me for now, and I could focus on moving forward with things with Darien. He was coming over for brunch tomorrow morning. He wanted to take me out, but I told him we needed to talk in private. He seemed a little concerned about that, but I told him not to be. Even though I was nervous about my talk with Darien, I knew what I was going to do it with, or without him, so I was able to drift into a peaceful sleep.

Chapter 21

Darien

As I drove to Toni's house, I was a little anxious about what she needed to talk to me about. I was just thinking the other day about how different she was from other women I've dated. She does not pressure me for a relationship. Then she calls and all but demands that I come home this weekend and now the face-to-face talk in private. Normally, I would run the other way from these situations. Toni was different, and I really liked her. I talked to Vince last night and he and Gina are moving forward with their wedding plans. The wedding is in five weeks. I plan to invite Toni, as my date. I told Vince about how things were going and how I was feeling about Toni. Of course, he had to tease me, but he said to watch myself, because it sounded like I was falling in love. He said a man in love is a dangerous creature. Thinking about that comment made me laugh. The thought of me being in love was enough to make anyone laugh out loud who really knew me. I remember how much Toni liked the flowers I bought her last weekend, so I stopped to get some more.

I was so excited about seeing her today, even though I didn't know what she wanted to talk about. I pulled in front of her house and walked up to the door. When I rang the doorbell and she opened the door, she looked so radiant it astounded me. She smiled when she saw the flowers and stepped aside to let me in. I gave her a half hug and a kiss on the cheek. I really wanted to do much more, but she seemed a little tense.

Toni

When I woke up this morning, I was a little more nervous about my talk with Darien. I kept trying to determine where to start with him. I wanted to let him know about the baby we were having, and I wanted to let him know about the baby I gave up seven years ago. There was so much I just didn't know where to begin. When he arrived, looking as fine as ever, carrying those beautiful flowers, everything I had rehearsed went out the window. I was back to square one being tongue-tied. I took my flowers and put them in some water in the kitchen while Darien went into the living room. I had finished making brunch and had everything set on the table. We had never eaten at the table, so I called him into the dining room.

He came into the dining room, saw the food on the table, and said, "Girl, you sure now how to welcome a man home."

I smiled and started to fix him a plate. While I was doing this, he said, "Toni, my friend is getting married and I wanted to know if you would go with me to the wedding, as my date?"

I thought to myself he might be taking that invitation back shortly, but until then I would accept. "Sure, Darien I would love to go with you. When is it?"

He answered that it was in five weeks.

"Oh a fall wedding, that's great. Sure, I will go with you. Just get me the details, time and location."

I could not delay this any longer. I just started at the beginning, which was that I was pregnant and he was the father. I told him that I know he was probably thinking I was trying to trap him, but I assured him that I was not. I would like him to be in my life, and a part of the baby's life, but if he decided he didn't want to do that, I was okay with that. I told him I would even sign something releasing him of any parental rights, if he wanted me to. I really wanted him to understand that I was not trying to gain financially by this, and I really like him and hoped we could work through this together. I decided not to go into the Benjamin prior pregnancy thing right now. That could come later, if he decided to stick this thing out with me. The entire time I was talking, I do not think he moved a muscle or blinked. In fact, I do not think he took a breath. At some point, I stopped to check and made sure that he was hearing everything I was telling him.

I said, "Darien are you okay?" He just nodded his head, yes. He didn't say anything. He just sat there staring into space. I got up and walked into the kitchen. My worst fear of him turning his back on me, was about to come true.

Darien

I could not believe what I was hearing. Toni was pregnant with my child. What was more unbelievable was my reaction to this news. Although I was shocked and was not prepared for this, my instinct was not to run in the other direction. I was fighting the urge to get down on one knee and ask her to marry me. Where in the hell was that coming from? My boy Vince was right. I must be in love because I was thinking about crazy stuff I never would have before. I realized that Toni had stopped talking, and she had actually gotten up to walk into the kitchen. I got up and followed her. She was standing at the counter with her head down. I walked up behind her, put my arms around her, and said, "Toni we will get through this together. Neither one of us wanted this to happen. We both went into this as adults saying we didn't want anything serious. Well making a baby together is pretty serious."

She chuckled through her tears. I continued, "We are just getting to know each other and we've got about nine months to finish getting to know each other before our child is born. I'm willing to stick it out with you if you will let me help you."

Toni turned around to face me and said, "Darien I swear I didn't mean for this to happen. The last thing I want you to think is that I tried to trap you by getting pregnant."

I put my finger up to her mouth to shush her and said "Toni, I know you're not that kind of girl. We were always very careful except for that one time. We both made the decision to have sex and we knew we didn't have any condoms. You never told me do not worry, I'm on the pill, or anything like that. You were honest with me. My issue with most women is that they're not honest. They're always trying to play games with men. I never felt that from you. I've always felt like everything you did or said was sincere." I pulled her to me and hugged her and I felt something for her in that moment that I've never felt for any woman before.

Chapter 22

Five weeks later
Toni

I woke up thinking about the wedding I was going to attend with Darien. His best friend Vincent was getting married to Gina. Darien had shared with me that Gina had gotten pregnant and he suspected that she had gotten pregnant on purpose to trap Vince. I had not had a chance to meet Vince, or Gina yet. Darien had been out of town trying to finish the business in Florida for the past few weeks. I was spending most of my spare time with Jada and the kids. She was doing better, but still in a lot of pain. She only took two weeks off work. I felt she should have taken more time. She said work helped keep her mind occupied. She took David Sr. up on his offer to come help with Tre. He was doing very well in therapy, and they expected him to make a full recovery. Jada had decided to take the kids to counseling to help them deal with David's death. She, too, had decided to seek counseling which I thought was an excellent idea.

I had not heard much more from Benjamin. He did get back to me to let me know that he intended to pursue trying to find the baby, I gave up, so he could determine if he is the father. I heard through Jada and David Sr. that he was doing well with his new job, so it seemed like he was

195

trying to get his life back on track. I did end up telling
Darien all about Benjamin one night, and he agreed that I
should probably try to find the baby to help Benjamin
determine paternity. He said he would want to know if he
had a child somewhere. I decided to give Benjamin as much
information as I could about the adoption agency to help in
his search. I let him know that if there was anything he
needed from me to help, to let me know.

Darien and I were still getting to know each other and
preparing for our baby. We went to our first prenatal
appointment together a couple of weeks ago, and he
promised he would go to all of them with me. We decided
not to rush into anything serious like living together. We
decided to set up a nursery at my house and one at his house
for now. We are taking things one day at a time. I did meet
his mother and sister, and that went well. He also met Jada,
and she seemed to like him also. Things were going well for
me right now. It almost does not seem fair that when things
seemed to be going well for Jada, my life was a mess, now
her life has taken a turn for the worse, and things seem to be
coming together for me. It would be nice for us both to be
happy at the same time, but unfortunately, life does not
work that way.

I finished getting ready for the wedding and headed
out. Darien was the best man, so he had to be at the church
early. He gave me directions and told me where to sit. He
would meet up with me at the reception. We would not be
able to sit together, but once the dancing started we could be
together. I arrived at the church and found a space to park. I
entered the church, found the usher, and told him who I
was. He showed me to my seat. Gina was white, so half of
the room was white, and the other half, which was Vincent's

friends and family, was black. It was somewhat funny to see the division of color in the room. I was pleasantly surprised when the music started to signal that the ceremony was about to begin. The groom and groomsmen came out and got into position. I saw Darien looking for me and when he saw me, he smiled. After I smiled back at him I looked over to get a good look at Vincent. I almost fell out of my chair. I was pretty sure Vincent, Darien's best friend, was Vinny from seven years ago. Oh, my God how could this be happening to me? I was trying to remain calm, but I was losing it. Darien looked over and mouthed to me, "You okay?"

I nodded my head, yes, and tried not to make eye contact with Vince. Luckily, he had not noticed me. When the bride walked in, it turns out that I knew her also.. Gina was the reporter who had interviewed David Jr. I shook my head as I though to myself, *what a small world.*

I made it through the ceremony and tried not to think about it. I kept stealing glances at Vince to confirm my fears, that he was in fact Vinny. I was going to have to try to figure out what to do before we all ended up at the reception together. I mean, maybe it was not a big deal that I might have had his best friend's baby seven years ago. Who was I kidding of course it was a big deal. This was a mess. I decided that I needed to try to get Darien alone to talk to him, before he introduced me to Vince. That was going to be almost impossible since he was the best man. He had all sorts of duties to perform as a part of the traditional wedding festivities.

Darien

I was very excited about today. I was happy for Vincent and Gina even though I thought she tricked him into marrying her, he did love her, so it really didn't matter how it happened. It was going to happen eventually anyway. I was also happy because I had decided I was going to ask Toni to marry me. We didn't have to get married before the baby, if she didn't want to, but I wanted her to know that I wanted to be in it for the long haul with her. Honestly, I was concerned about her ex, Benjamin, trying to come back into the picture, and I wanted it known that she was my woman now. In the back of my mind, I was worried that he would find the child she gave up. If it turned out that, he was the father maybe she would want to go back to him. I needed some insurance, like her being my wife, or at least engaged to be my wife. I had talked to Vince about it to make sure he would not be upset by me doing it during the reception. He was shocked, but happy for me. He was so supportive of my decision to try to make things work with Toni.

Toni

When I arrived at the reception, I was very nervous. I found my assigned table, which happened to be right up front, close to the bridal party table. I know Darien did that on purpose. I should have been in the back, since I didn't know anyone but him. I decided to roll with it. If Vince did recognize me, he would have to make a decision about telling Darien. There was always the chance he didn't remember, or recognize me. Just then, they announced that the wedding party had arrived. They announced the bride and groom as Mr. and Mrs. Smith, as Vincent and Gina walked in. Gina looked gorgeous, even though it was obvious she was pregnant, she looked wonderful in her white dress. Darien was looking for me, as he walked in and took his seat at the head table. He was sitting next to Vince, and I saw him motion towards me. I quickly turned my head the other way.

I knew it was only a matter of time before I would have to face Vince, because Darien was set on us meeting, understandably so. I was able to hide in the restroom through most of the festivities, but at some point Darien sent one of Gina's bridesmaids into the restroom to check on me. I told her I was okay and would be right out. When I walked out of the restroom, there stood Vince and Darien. When Vince looked at me, I knew instantly that he recognized me, but he didn't let on to Darien. I followed his lead and let Darien introduce us like we were complete strangers. After we met, Vince led Darien away, and I continued to watch them to see if I could tell what they were talking about.

Vince

I could not believe it. My boy Darien, had fallen in love with one of my ex girlfriends. According to him, it's possible that she had my child. How in the world was I going to tell him this? He was in love with her, and about to propose. I didn't want to ruin things for him, but he had to know the truth, so that he could decide how he wanted to proceed with things. Should I let him propose to her, or should I tell him now that Toni was the girl from college, I went out with a few times, but lost touch with. I decided to try to convince him to hold off on the proposal. I would not get into it tonight with him on why, because I didn't want anything to ruin the night for Gina. She didn't need any added stress or drama tonight. Her parents were giving her enough grief about marrying me in the first place. All we needed was some ghetto drama kicking off at the reception, and they would be saying I told you so from now until the end of time.

Toni

I thought about what Darien said the night I told him about me being pregnant. He said that I had always been honest with him and he trusted me. I remembered those words and my decision was made. I had to find Darien right now and tell him the truth about Vince. I could not risk Vince telling him first and him losing his trust in me. I saw Darien across the room talking to some other people. I started towards him. Out of the corner of my eye, I saw Vince heading towards him as well. I picked up my pace and I made it to him first. I touched his shoulder and asked if I could speak with him alone outside. Just then, Vince walked up and said, "Hey, Darien can I speak to you for a minute?"

Darien looked at me, then back at Vince, and said, "Hey man, I need to go outside with Toni for a minute. I'll holler at you in a minute, when I get back."

Vince looked a little nervous but he agreed.

When we got outside Darien pulled me to him to hug and kiss me. I pulled back and said, "Darien we have to talk."

He seemed alarmed by my tone and stepped back and said, "Toni what's wrong? Did I do something wrong?"

I shook my head no, and said, "No Darien, you have done nothing wrong, but I have to tell you something now."

"Okay" he said, "What is so important that it can't wait until later?"

I said, "Darien your friend Vince is Vinny from seven years ago." I could tell that he was processing what I had just said to him, but he didn't say anything. "I knew him as Vinny and never knew his last name. You always referred to him as Vince. I never thought we were talking about the same person."

Finally, he said, "Toni stop, please. Why do you always think I will not believe you? Listen this is a little bit of a shock, but we can deal with this okay? I just need some time to process this, and I need to talk to Vince. Do you think he remembers you?"

I nodded my head, yes, and said, "Yes I'm sure he remembers me. I could tell as soon as you introduced us."

He thought for a minute and then said, "Well listen I'm glad you told me babe, but this doesn't change anything for me. I just need to talk to Vince, to make sure he does not have an issue with this, and we will take it from there. Okay? I might not get a chance to talk to him about it tonight."

I cut him off and said, "Oh, I think you will."

I saw Vince standing at the door watching us the entire time. "I think he wants to talk to you now." I motioned towards the door and he turned and saw Vince standing there. I said, "Let me go inside and the two of you can talk."

He nodded, yes, and I headed towards the door. When I reached the door, Vince was standing there and I said, "I already told him and he wants to talk to you now."

Vince didn't say anything he just headed towards Darien.

Vince

I walked up to Darien and his back was turned to me. I had no idea that his frame of mind was at this point. I called his name and he turned around. I started to talk, but he put his hand up and said, "Vince I've known you a long time. I've never loved a woman like I love Toni. I want to be with her and raise our child together. She just told me that you and she were together back in college. I can deal with that as long as you can. I mean as long as you understand she's mine now, and no matter if you find out that the child she had was yours, you cannot have that type of relationship with her ever again."

I was very surprised by Darien's tone with me. I hesitated for a minute after he finished and collected my thoughts before I responded. Finally, I said, "Darien I understand what it feels like to love a woman so much that nothing matters. I do not have a problem with you being with Toni. She is a great girl and I'm not interested in pursuing anything more than a friendship with her. Even if Benjamin finds the child and determines that, he is not the father. That would mean the child was mine and it would not change anything for me. I love Gina and plan to start my life with her tonight. I will not be thinking about any other women from this point forward."

After I finished Darien gave me a big bear hug and then said, "Man I'm going in here to propose to my girl. I love her. I can't believe I'm saying that, but I do, and I don't want to make the mistake of losing her."

I patted my friend on the back and said, "I understand how you feel. Go do your thing."

Toni

I was nervously waiting for Darien and Vince to re-appear. I went back into the reception hall to get some punch and to sit down to rest my feet. I didn't see them walk back into the room, but the next thing I knew the band had stopped playing and Darien had the microphone. I wondered what he was doing because he had already done the traditional toast. Darien said, "Excuse me everyone. I would like to have everyone's attention. I know we are all here to celebrate the union of Gina and Vince. However, I would like to take just one moment to ask the lady in my life an important question." I almost spit my punch out all over the table. "Toni baby please come join me on the stage."

I was shaking my head, no, but he insisted, "Come on now baby. Don't make me come down there to get you."

I could not believe he was doing this to me. I guess the best part about it was I really didn't know any of these people, but as soon as I said that, I felt a tap on my shoulder and saw Jada standing there behind me.

I turned and said, "Girl what are you doing here?"

She just smiled and said, "Toni go up on the stage please."

I protested the entire way, but did as I was told. When I reached the stage, Darien brought me closer to him and then dropped down on one knee. I gasped and brought my hand to my mouth. He looked at me and said, "Toni will you please give me the honor of being my wife?"

The crowd was cheering and I saw Jada clapping and crying. She was nodding her head, yes. I turned to Darien and through tears, I said, "yes."

Darien jumped up, picked me up, and twirled me around. The band started playing our song, which was, *The First Time Ever I Saw Your Face*. Darien looked me in my eyes and said, "Toni, I love you. I've never loved anyone before you and I will not after you. You're the only woman for me."

I could not believe my ears. Darien had never told me he loved me before. I loved him but had never told him either. I was crying so hard now, but I managed to say, "Baby, I love you, too."

Yesterday's Lies

Discussion Questions

1. How would you feel if your best friend kept a secret from you like Toni and Jada did from each other?
2. Do you think your friendship could survive something like this?
3. What do you think about how Toni handled the situation with her pregnancy in college? Do you think she did the right thing by going off on her own or was that selfish of her?
4. What do you think about David Jr. allowing Benjamin to go to jail for him?
5. Do you think Benjamin took the blame because he felt he owed David's family for taking him in?
6. How did you feel about David Sr.'s controlling actions when Benjamin was released from jail?
7. How did you feel about Toni's reaction to Benjamin's return?
8. Which character do you feel had the most impact on the story?
9. Which character was your favorite and why?

10. Have you ever kept a journal? If so what types of things did you write about?
11. How did you feel about how Darien handled Vince when he was upset about Gina being pregnant?
12. Do you think Gina trapped Vince on purpose?
13. Do you think Toni was jealous of Jada and David Jr. marriage?
14. An overall thought on the book and the authors writing style.